Dearest Ericka,

Your father and I grew up together in Connecticut and were roommates at West Point. He was the finest of men, the bravest of soldiers, and I was proud to call him my closest friend. Either of us would have given his life for the other, but I am getting ahead of myself.

I always felt a great loyalty to my parents' country, Vashmira. Perhaps because my family comes from royal blood, I felt a great sense of duty to my people. I returned to Vashmira to aid my country in our fight for independence. Out of loyalty to me, your father took on my cause.

Our fight succeeded in freeing my people, but the cost was high. During the fiercest of battles, your father suffered a grievous wound while guarding my back. Before he died in my arms, we pledged to one another that our firstborn children, Nicholas and Ericka, would one day wed. It is my most fervent wish that our children fulfill a man's promise to his dying friend.

Sincerely,

His Royal Highness of Vashmira, King Zared I

Dear Reader,

My parents took our family on fabulous vacations: skiing in New Jersey and Vermont, sailing in the Bahamas and the Caribbean, horseback riding in the Catskills and camping in the Pennsylvania mountains. As a result, I've developed a lifelong love of travel. After college I visited Canada, Europe, Asia and much of the United States. I still find meeting new people and experiencing new cultures fascinating.

So what could be better than creating my very own country for readers to share with me? Or writing about that country's royal family? THE CROWN AFFAIR trilogy begins with *Royal Target* and King Nicholas Zared, a man determined to hold his country together—even if the price is marrying American Ericka Allen. As danger swirls around the couple, neither of them is sure whom to trust.

I hope you'll get caught up in their romantic story enough to drop me a note. I love to hear from readers, and you can reach me at my Web site www.SusanKearney.com.

Susan Kea

ROYAL TARGET
SUSAN KEARNEY

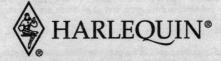

HARLEQUIN®

TORONTO • NEW YORK • LONDON
AMSTERDAM • PARIS • SYDNEY • HAMBURG
STOCKHOLM • ATHENS • TOKYO • MILAN • MADRID
PRAGUE • WARSAW • BUDAPEST • AUCKLAND

ISBN 0-373-22682-9

ROYAL TARGET

This edition published by arrangement with Harlequin Books S.A.

® and TM are trademarks of the publisher. Trademarks indicated with
® are registered in the United States Patent and Trademark Office, the
Canadian Trade Marks Office and in other countries.

Visit us at www.eHarlequin.com

Printed in U.S.A.

ABOUT THE AUTHOR

Susan Kearney used to set herself on fire four times a day. Now she does something really hot—she writes romantic suspense. While she no longer performs her signature fire dive (she's taken up figure skating), she never runs out of ideas for characters and plots. A business graduate from the University of Michigan, Susan writes full-time. She resides in a small town outside Tampa, Florida, with her husband and children and a spoiled Boston terrier. Visit her at http://www.SusanKearney.com.

Books by Susan Kearney

THE ZAREDS

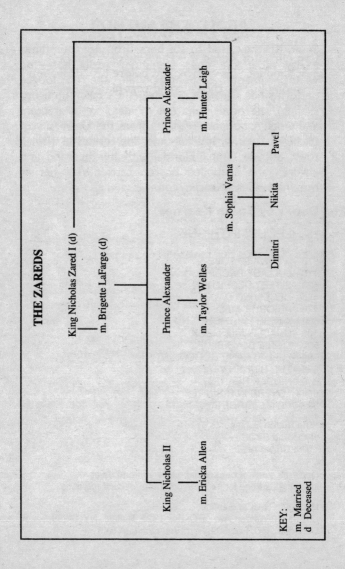

King Nicholas Zared I (d)
m. Brigette LaFarge (d)

King Nicholas II
m. Ericka Allen

Prince Alexander
m. Taylor Welles

Prince Alexander
m. Hunter Leigh
m. Sophia Varna

Dimitri   Nikita   Pavel

KEY:
m. Married
d Deceased

CAST OF CHARACTERS

King Nicholas Zared II—The King of Vashmira must announce his engagement before his coronation ceremony. But his choice could cost him his heart—and his life....

Ericka Allen—An American reporter promised by law to the King of Vashmira, a darkly handsome ruler whom she has never met and has no intention of yielding to....

Princess Tashya Zared—She's worried about her eldest brother. Someone is out to kill him...and maybe the entire royal family, too.

Sophia Varna Zared—The king's stepmother seems to be mourning her husband's death, but is she as sincere as she appears?

General Levsky Vladimir—He has the Vashmiran military in the palm of his hand, but is his loyalty to the crown?

Ira Hanuck—Who better to carry out an assassination attempt than the Chief of Palace Security?

Larissa Belosova—She was once Nicholas's lady friend and seemed destined to rule by his side. Has she accepted his decision to marry the American beauty, or is she out for revenge...?

For Vivan Ducas
a special thanks for your creative vision.

Prologue

"It's time you married the bride I chose for you, Nicholas," King Zared I said, as he raised his sharp gaze from the documents on his sixteenth-century antique desk and scowled at his son.

Not again. At least once a year his dad summoned Nicholas to his royal office and pressed him to marry. Annoyed by his father's persistence, Nicholas refrained from rolling his eyes at the ceiling, and instead glanced back at the man with whom he found it so difficult to argue.

At fifty, hair black as midnight but short and neat, his shoulders still broad and firm, Zared looked every inch a king. But it was more than his height, his regal demeanor and a sharp wit that had won the admiration of Vashmira's loyal subjects; Zared was the hero of their revolution.

Not only had the king attained hero status during his lifetime, he had earned the love and respect of his family. Zared always meant well and because Nicholas loved his father, he found it difficult to reject the request, but he fully intended to hold his ground again. "I should be working."

"So should I." His father grinned, the charm that mesmerized millions of their people softening his words. "Although making you to listen to me is the hardest work I've done all year."

Nicholas didn't argue with the exaggeration. His father could outwork most farmhands, dance the night away like a Cossack and still run five miles with elite palace security officers in the morning. Unwilling to overreact, Nicholas concentrated on remaining composed and looked out the palace window into the private courtyard.

A few moths fluttered close to the golden-hued lamplights above iron-studded gates. Mosquitoes buzzed incessantly and recycled water gurgled in the fountains. The sweet aroma of scarlet pelargoniums wafted through the air.

Calmed, he faced his father again and responded mildly to his complaint. "I always listen."

"And then you do exactly what *you* want." His father slapped his palm onto his desk, scattering documents. "It's high time you and Ericka Allen meet, fall in love and marry."

Nicholas identified his father's obstinate I-am-the-king-so-obey-me parenting technique. Avoiding the unpalatable topic of his arranged marriage wasn't going to work. He slipped into a well-worn leather chair, laced his fingers behind his head and tried not to express his frustration. As heir to the throne of Vashmira, he willingly fulfilled most of the obligations required of him, accepting that he would be asked to meet the needs of his people in numerous capacities—but marrying a stranger pushed the limits of loyalty and duty to country.

Nicholas strove to sound reasonable. "Just because her father died saving your life doesn't mean she'll want to have anything to do with me or the contract you cooked up with your old friend."

"Her father was like a brother to me."

Nicholas looked out a window and watched the wind brushing a tufted box shrub against the ivy-covered brick of the inner courtyard. The shrubs needed trimming. Nicholas loathed the subject of their conversation so much that he was willing to distract himself, however, with watching the shrubs' shadows shift against the wall.

While he admired his father's devotion to his old friend who'd died protecting him, he understood both the advantages and disadvantages of marriage to an American. An American-born princess bride could almost assure his country of increased economic aid from the United States and favorable loans from the International Monetary Fund, especially if the American was Ericka Allen, a highly respected correspondent for a major newspaper who had access to many powerful men in her government. However, stronger American connections would find disfavor among many of his people who preferred the old ways.

On a personal level, he was fairly certain that Ericka Allen was not in favor of their union, and the last thing he wanted was an unwilling bride. Over the years his father had sent her family funds and kept tabs on the woman. Although she had known about the contract since her eighteenth birthday when his father had written her, she had never bothered to contact them—which stung his pride a little. Obviously, she wasn't interested, a fact he'd mentioned to the king before—to no avail.

Grimly, he reminded himself there was some wiggle room. The lady could back out. So could he—but at the risk of destabilizing his country. If he chose another woman, many political factors would come into play. Some as simple as which language dominated Vashmira's communications and trade. Born of noble Russian parents who'd immigrated to the United States, King Zared I spoke English, Russian and Arabic, the three official languages of Vashmira, and he'd insisted that his children learn them, too. Many of their citizens resisted learning all three languages, contending the rest of the country should convert to their preference.

Just as different languages separated Vashmira's people, so did the three main religions of Christianity, Judaism and Islam. Religious leaders would evaluate and assess Nicholas' wife with their own partisan agendas in mind. He had to select his queen with caution, insult no one—but the best way to accomplish that task was to adhere to his father's wishes, since Zared was beloved by all factions. Nicholas was caught in a bureaucratic trap of his father's creation.

Unfortunately, nothing Nicholas said seemed to make one iota of difference in changing his father's mind. Nicholas secretly hoped if he simply delayed long enough, Ericka Allen would eventually marry another man and let him off the hook.

However, he kept the thought to himself. "I understand arranged marriage contracts are prohibited in the United States."

"Last time I checked, we live in Vashmira, where such marriage contracts *are* legal. Since I am the king, and I uphold the laws, and you are a citizen, you will obey them. Invite her over for a visit."

"No."

"Fine. I'll ask her myself."

"Next week would be good. I'll be in Cairo then for the Mid-East peace talks."

His father leaned forward and crossed his arms over his chest. "Why are you fighting me?"

Nicholas knew better than to give a political reason as an answer. "You of all men should understand. You married my mother for love. After she died, you married Sophia for love. I simply wish to do the same."

His father's eyes twinkled. "There is no reason you cannot love my friend's daughter."

Nicholas groaned and shoved to his feet. Retreating might be his best bet. Quarreling with the king was always complicated, especially when his father used his own singular brand of logic and charm. "You never give up, do you, Father?"

"I never stop fighting for our people. An alliance with the West is critical to our survival. Without the hard dollars of American currency, we cannot feed and educate our children. I'm hoping Ericka Allen will do for Vashmira what Princess Grace did for Monaco and what Queen Noor did for Jordan. Her illustrious political connections will prove invaluable to us. A woman in her position will know the ins and outs of the congressional system, how best to acquire economic aid and loans. An American princess will put our country on the map.''

''Father, I really have work to do.'' Nicholas strode out of the office, the heat of his irritation chilled by his father's persistence and the knowledge that his arguments did have political merit. However, surely the discussion was over for another year?

Nicholas strode through the royal foyer, and the palace guards closed the doors behind him. He had not yet departed the outer reception area when the loud crack of a gunshot sounded behind him.

Nicholas' heartbeat galloped and he broke into a sweat. The shot sounded as if it had come from his father's office! Adrenaline and fear spurring him, he rushed past the guards into the royal office. They followed close on his heels. No one else was there— except his father—who lay on the floor in a puddle of blood.

So much blood.

''Find the man who did this,'' Nicholas ordered, outrage hot upon him even as he searched for a pulse. But his father's bright blue eyes had already turned glassy. His heart no longer beat.

In shock, Nicholas cradled his father, rocking him, unable to shed the tears scalding his eyes and constricting his throat or release the sobs bottled in his chest. As his father's body chilled, he vowed to find his killer.

From deep inside, he drew on a strength he'd never known he had. It took enormous effort to force his fingers to uncurl and disengage from his father's body.

Finally, he shoved to his feet, struggling with the weight of guilt and grief and the burden of new responsibilities. With a heavy heart, he went to inform and console his stepmother and siblings.

Their king was dead.

Chapter One

One Year Later

"I'm sending you to Vashmira." Larry Hogan, Ericka's boss, senior editor and friend at the *Washington Herald*, strode into her cubbyhole of an office and beamed at her, looking as if he'd just assigned her the scoop of the century. His smile gleamed almost as brightly as his bald head and his green eyes sparkled with humor.

At the mention of Vashmira, Ericka Allen stiffened, her lungs deflated like a popped balloon. She'd known the name of that country before she'd learned the Pledge of Allegiance. "I can't go there."

"Of course you'll go. We'll send the photographer over later for Nicholas Zared II's coronation ceremony. You've got an exclusive interview with him."

Hogan had just slotted her the assignment of a lifetime. Despite her need to refuse, for a moment she couldn't tamp down her excitement. This was a one-in-a-million opportunity. Her private take on the coronation for the American public would shape the thoughts of millions of readers. AP and UPI would pick up a story of this magnitude, and her byline would be splashed across every newspaper in America.

Still, when her editor tossed the round-trip airline ticket to Vashmira on her computer keyboard, Ericka arched a suspicious eyebrow. "Why do we rate an exclusive interview?"

"Our paper is owned by the Randall Foundation."

Which, Ericka knew, included a conglomerate of newspapers, television and radio stations and several publishing companies. "The Randall Foundation has ties to Vashmira?"

"Apparently we're thinking of launching communication satellites from Vashmira. Zared wants our business."

Ericka nodded, still not convinced her exclusive hadn't been orchestrated for other purposes. Although a few stories had very occasionally fallen into her lap, it didn't happen often, increasing her suspicions. "Who chose me for this assignment?"

"I did." Hogan nudged the ticket into her lap. "Say, thank you."

She should say *no*.

Ambition warred with an inherent caution. While Ericka coveted the exclusive interview, her instincts screamed to run fast and hard and without stopping in the opposite direction. This assignment wasn't due to some foreign politician requesting her to interview him because he liked her prose. Although she wasn't above accepting assignments that came her way due to her hard work, intelligence and courtesy and had no compunction about using connections that she'd carefully built up over the years to obtain a story, she sensed Vashmira's newest leader might want her for reasons other than her work.

"I can't go."

"You're kidding, right?" Hogan's eyes narrowed to emerald chips of glass. "You used to beg me to send you on assignments from Baghdad to war-torn Bosnia. You've covered every two-bit dictator and most heads of state in Europe and Asia during the last ten years, and now, you don't want to go?"

"No."

"You're sick?"

"No."

Hogan glared at her. "Pregnant?"

"Don't be silly. I've been covering our presidential election." As she'd moved up the career ladder, she'd willingly paid the price for success and had never looked back. Her personal life had suffered, and she'd lost track of most of her old friends. She couldn't remember the last time she'd had a date. "For months now, I haven't been in one city for more than a night at a time."

"Last I heard, it only takes one time."

Exasperation entered her tone. "Hogan, I am *not* pregnant."

"Fine, then. Have a good flight. I'll see you after you return." His pager beeped, his cell phone rang. He started to take the call as if the conversation was over.

Ericka stood and placed her hand over his. "Can you keep a secret?"

Curiosity burning in his eyes, Hogan frowned at her and ignored his call. "What have you done now?"

"Look, I have ties to Vashmira that go back almost three decades. It may not be safe for me to…"

Like any good newsman, Hogan could smell a hot story a mile away. And hers was a doozy. "What kind of ties?"

"My father died saving King Zared's life during the war for Vashmira's independence."

Her mother had told the story like a fairy tale, with great flair and drama, but she could not change the fact that her husband had run off on an adventure, risking his life and virtually abandoning his wife and baby daughter. Ericka told herself for the thousandth time that her father had expected to come back to them, but as an adult she still couldn't banish the old hurt from her childhood or the feelings of abandonment.

"I'm sorry, Ericka. I knew he died when you were a baby, but I didn't know he was in Vashmira."

"To repay us for my father's loyalty, King Zared sent my mother and me a monthly stipend that helped keep a roof over our heads."

"That was kind of the king, but I don't see the problem."

"There was no other contact between the Zareds and us until my senior year of high school."

Hogan stuck his head out of her door and yelled to her secretary. "No interruptions."

"Yes, sir."

He closed the door, helped himself to a cup of coffee and perched a hip on the corner of her desk, giving her time to gather her spinning thoughts. Ericka swallowed hard, her throat tight with tension.

"On my eighteenth birthday, I received an official-looking package. Purple ribbons made the wax-sealed letter look important; the thick, yellow vellum seemed to indicate the passage of time."

"King Zared sent you something from your father?"

"When I saw the bold, masculine scrawl of my name across the inner envelope, I hoped so." She could still recall how her heart rate had jumped just from holding the envelope in her hand. Although her father had died when she was a baby, she'd never given up hoping for a personal message from him, a videotape, a diary, even a letter, but there had been nothing except the occasional fond remembrance from her mother.

"What did it say?"

"I still remember the letter word for word.

Dearest Ericka,
Your father, Erick, and I grew up together in Connecticut, attended the same prep school and were roommates at West Point, but we were much more than comrades. Although we were not related by blood, I loved your father like a brother. He was the finest of men, the bravest of soldiers, and I was proud to call him my closest friend. Either of us would have given his life for the other, but I am getting ahead of myself.

Although I was an American citizen, I always felt a great loyalty to my parents' country, Vashmira. Perhaps because my family comes from royal blood, I felt a great sense of duty and responsibility to my people. I felt compelled to return to Vashmira and aid my country in our fight for independence. Out of loyalty to me, your father took on my cause as his own.

Our fight succeeded in freeing my people from the dictatorship of communism, but the cost was very high. During the fiercest of battles, your father suffered a grievous wound while guarding my back. Before he died in my arms, we pledged to one another that our firstborn children, Nicholas Zared II and Ericka Allen would one day wed. It is my most fervent wish that our children fulfill a man's promise to his dying friend.

Sincerely,
His Royal Highness of Vashmira, King Zared I''

Even in high school Ericka had found the notion of marriage unacceptable. She'd intended to remain single and independent, at the beck and call of no one. The idea of an arranged marriage to a man she'd never met was outrageously medieval, simply out of the question. Women were not property to be owned or traded for the sake of ancient promises—no matter how much some men wanted to think so.

Besides, who could visualize her as a queen? What a hoot.

Although she'd never been interested, she had been curious. She'd seen pictures of Nicholas Zared II, studied his features with both fascination and self-disgust at that fascination. The strong jaw, the straight white teeth, the kingly set of his shoulders called to her on a level she didn't want to acknowledge. Although the expression on Nicholas Zared II's handsome face was arrogant, intelligence gleamed from his eyes, and she'd wondered what he thought about their fathers' scheme to get them together.

"You saved the letter?" Hogan asked.

She nodded. "In my safe-deposit box. I never answered King Zared. The year after high school, I worked all summer, attended college in the fall, and you know the rest."

She and Hogan had been together a long time. He knew she'd worked her way through college, where she'd studied political journalism, and had landed a job with a weekly publication right after graduation. She'd made her career by begging for assignments in dangerous places, willing to enter hot zones to get a story. Hogan knew her ultimate goal of some day writing political thrillers. But that goal still remained a long way off. Over the years she'd built an impressive network of contacts and now worked for him at one of Washington's most respected papers.

"That's some story."

"When I first left the United States on assignment to Europe, I worried the Vashmiran government might try to coerce me into honoring the marriage contract."

"You're still here. Single." He stated the obvious.

"And ten years have passed without any further contact. I figured I was free, the old contract forgotten. But now, I'm not so sure."

"Zared I died last year. You think his son is making a move on you?"

Like all political analysts, Ericka kept up on international news, taking particular notice of Vashmira after King Zared I's assassination. His firstborn son had stepped into his father's shoes quite admirably. He'd kept the monetary and political system stable, an achievement worthy of notice in that part of the world. It bothered her that he hadn't yet announced whom he would marry, a requirement of Vashmiran law he must fulfill to ascend the throne, but he'd never contacted her, either. Nevertheless, the prospect of going to Vashmira to cover the coronation troubled her.

"You think the exclusive interview is simply bait to get you to Vashmira?"

The idea sounded not just far-fetched but preposterous when Hogan voiced her thoughts aloud.

Yet of all the reporters in the United States, she'd been handed an opportunity as rare as a six-figure advance for a first-time novelist. "I don't believe in coincidences."

"But?" he prodded.

Despite her concerns, she yearned to see the country her father had given his life for. Those stories her mother had told her so long ago had made her curious about the country and its people. "I have no intention of jeopardizing my job, my friends or my citizenship to satisfy a childhood curiosity or to write a story."

"The paper can provide you with protection."

"Who can be sent back at the border."

"Have you had an attorney—"

She was a step ahead of him. "The contract isn't binding in the United States, but my lawyer is sure it's legal in Vashmira."

"No modern king would resort to forcing an American to marry him. And we could take precautions by informing the U.S. ambassador of your presence and intention to leave Vashmira at the completion of your assignment."

"An embassy only has limited powers in foreign countries," she reminded him, having already considered all the angles.

"Look, even if I was willing to send another reporter, no one else is free. No one else has your experience or knows the territory better. And now you have an inside track. If you refuse this assignment, I'll have to fire you."

"What?" His words stunned her. She hadn't even considered that she'd be given an ultimatum.

"I'm sorry, but your excuses won't wash with management. They might be sympathetic to your problem, but to them, the coronation story is the bottom line. Besides, are you sure the younger Zared even knows about the old marriage contract?"

Thoughts swirling, gut churning, she shrugged. "I'm not sure of anything."

Chapter Two

Ericka could be flying straight into danger, she thought as the flight attendant handed her a glass of orange juice. Yet she preferred the risk to being fired if she refused the assignment. She'd taken more serious risks flying into war-torn countries or traipsing into hot zones where she could have been kidnapped, raped or killed. The worst thing that could happen to her in Vashmira was a trip to the pokey for refusing to honor a ridiculous marriage contract. The bad publicity alone that such a move would attract would more than likely ensure her freedom. Vashmira was a new country struggling to exist in the modern world. Arresting her would be counterproductive at best and stupid at worst. Besides, she could hardly blame her boss. She *was* the most experienced reporter on staff. Two of the three other correspondents capable of taking over were on assignment, one in Africa, the other at the Middle-East peace talks in Jordan, the third on vacation in the Australian outback. Which left her in the lurch.

She'd briefly considered refusing the assignment and finding another job even if it meant taking a step backward in her career, but if the Vashmiran government really intended to kidnap her, they could have hired a mercenary to come after her. Since she'd had no problems, her marriage contract had probably been long forgotten. Even if Nicholas remembered the old agreement, she couldn't conceive of him wanting to marry a stranger. He was royalty, no doubt accustomed to women throwing themselves at him, something she had way too much self-respect ever to do.

After changing planes in Munich yesterday, she'd flown to Istanbul and slept through the night in a hotel there, recovering from jet lag before catching a short flight north into Vashmira this morning. Having finished her juice, she peered out the airplane's window and was disappointed by thick cloud cover that hid the ground. Taking out her laptop, she intended to scan her extensive files, but couldn't concentrate. Flying normally relaxed her, but she was unable to contain her mixture of excitement and trepidation. This was the story of any reporter's dreams, and she hadn't been able to resist the opportunity, not just to further her career, but for more personal reasons. She yearned to see the country her father had given his life for and possibly to add to his legacy by writing about Vashmira and introducing the country to the West.

She had no patience for the mountains of political, historical and geographical data in her laptop and found herself once again preoccupied with a picture of Nicholas Zared's face on her screen. What kind of man was he? He looked as if he'd brushed his hair for the picture, then impatient, raggedly run his fingers through it. His face was all aristocratic lines and noble angles—eyebrows, mouth, nose, looked European, royal, almost arrogant except for the glimmer of mirth in his eyes. Ericka didn't mind arrogance. She possessed plenty of that herself.

Arrogance helped her interview world leaders, dictators and royalty. She took pride in her job, in doing it well by telling her stories so that her readers felt as if they were there in the room with her. She asked the questions her readers wanted to ask themselves without suffering the discomforts of traveling halfway around the world for answers.

While her readers would appreciate Nicholas' handsome face as much as she did, it was unlike her to become so fascinated with her subject matter. But this story, this country, had more personal ramifications than usual.

Annoyed with her absorption in Nicholas' features, she snapped her laptop closed and prepared for landing. The flight attendant repeated instructions in Russian and English in which she was fluent, and Arabic, of which she couldn't understand a word.

In the modest but modern Vashmiran airport, all signs were painted in those same three languages. She headed briskly toward baggage, then paused in puzzlement when she spied a tall, broad-shouldered man, a cap low over his forehead, holding up a sign with her name. Neither she nor her newspaper had requested the services of a guide, since she'd been invited to stay at the palace.

She almost strolled right by, until she got a look at the man's distinctive visage. King Nicholas Zared! After just studying his computer picture, she could not be mistaken. Yet why was the king dressed in the rough clothing of a taxi driver? Why was he holding up a sign with her name on it? And why was he eyeing her with a look of a tiger about to pounce?

She almost halted in her tracks, but because it amused her, she decided to play along with his ruse. She approached him, warily, taking in not just the king, but a team of security guards who tried and failed to blend in with the crowd of travellers as they kept back onlookers. She told herself her quickened pulse was from his surprise tactics, not due to the striking man himself.

Just because up close and personal he was so much better looking than his picture was no reason to come unglued. After all, she'd interviewed the U.S. president and Mel Gibson. No worldwide celebrity, Zared was merely head of a very minor country. However the word "merely" seemed much too understated to apply to anything concerning Nicholas Zared. Larger than ordinary men, he had a commanding presence. And neither a long plane ride nor his assumption of her stupidity could account for the tingle of awareness she felt zinging through her veins when she approached him.

Did he think her so dense she wouldn't recognize the man she'd been assigned to interview? What game was he playing? Even as she wondered whether she should be insulted or not, wary or not, she couldn't help feeling amused.

"I'm Ericka Allen," she told him, willing to go along for now. One glance and he shot the full impact of his personality at her. Intense. Focused. Interested.

He looked at her like any man sizing up a woman. She read his interest in the arrogant tilt of his head, in the way he surveyed her from head to toe as though he had the right to judge her.

He would soon learn that this American woman had come here to work—not play. She had to balance her moves as if she were on a tightwire—remain friendly in order to obtain her critical interview and reject any advances in such a way that he believed he was the one doing the rejecting. To manage this, she couldn't reveal that she recognized his personal interest in her. At the same time she had to do some serious risk evaluation. She needed to discover whether he'd forgotten about the old marriage contract or remembered it but had no intention of honoring it. Holding his gaze, she smiled at him warmly. It was a smile she'd practiced—personal, but not too inviting.

In person, she found his face more compelling, bolder and more riveting than the picture on her computer screen. Although she was here to work, she saw no reason why she couldn't appreciate his looks. The longer their eyes held, the more she wondered what he was thinking. Reportedly, he was a master at keeping his thoughts locked up, hidden. A little work, a little easygoing conversation might be a good thing. No harm in some small talk while she took the measure of the man.

"The king has sent a car to take you to the palace." His words were truthful but misleading and spoken in a deep tone that spiked a shiver of pure womanly appreciation.

"That's very kind of the king." She widened her eyes innocently. "And you are?"

"Among other things," he tipped his hat and flashed her a charming grin, "your driver. My friends call me Nick."

A killer smile. A hunky build. And he seemed most polite. No doubt about it. He was wealthy, powerful and about to be crowned king. A girl could do worse. And once the photographer took his picture and her story made headlines, his worldwide popularity would soar. If he wasn't already, he'd be fending off women with a sword.

"Nick." She sent him her most pleasant smile and ignored the fact that he couldn't seem to take his gaze off her face, ignored the way her breath seemed to catch, ignored the lightness of her step. She knew what it meant when a man studied her that way, but she pretended she was unaware of his interest in her as a woman.

This game was one she was an expert at, a game she played to win—which meant obtaining her story, getting him to open up and trust her, without permitting their situation to become personal. Accustomed to offers from men, she understood the steps necessary to evade entanglement.

She and Nicholas walked through the terminal side by side, and she pretended not to notice how his security guards cleared a path for them. While she thought his ruse silly, she felt a certain amusement in his having taken so much trouble to disguise himself, although she still couldn't figure out why.

Actually meeting under these informal circumstances, without the presence of his formidable family or ministers of state, would allow her to gauge his character more easily. A bit impressed that he wasn't already talking about himself, she glanced at him again. A taxi driver's uniform couldn't hide his commanding presence any more than she could curtail her burgeoning curiosity. And, all-male animal that he was, he was responding to her interest with a smoky glance, his eyes pleased and full of mischief.

When he turned to exit the terminal, she halted. "My baggage?"

"Will be delivered to the palace."

His tone suggested that they weren't going to the palace, at least not straightaway, and that he expected her to ask questions. Ericka understood that the best way to get a man to talk was often to say nothing at all. So she simply waited for him to explain his plans.

A man like Nicholas always had plans. She could practically see them swirling in his mind. Ericka enjoyed a thinking man, one who could take charge as easily as he breathed, a man like Nicholas who wouldn't feel threatened by her intelligence or good looks. Powerful men were usually so wrapped up in their work that they were often inconsiderate, selfish with their time and their feelings and couldn't even make decent dinner conversation, never mind an enjoyable companion for a week.

They ambled outside past double glass doors, stopping beside a spit-shined black Mercedes, which was parked in a no-parking zone. Two guards gestured the crowds back. A cop suggested that travellers use another entrance.

Chivalrously, Nicholas took her elbow, his touch light, but not impersonal. So why did she feel as nervous as a rookie journalist on her first story?

He opened the front passenger door of the Mercedes for her with a polite and graceful ease. "Would you like to sightsee or go straight to the palace?"

She slipped into the cool, elegant leather seat. "A drive would be great, and maybe a walk, please, to get my bearings."

Nicholas shut her door, strode around the car and took the driver's seat. She watched him shift into gear, admiring the coordination of his hand on the gearshift, one foot on the clutch, the other on the brake. Clearly, he was accustomed to driving, another surprise. Most heads of state had a driver and preferred the luxury and status of being driven.

She hoped he wasn't one of those men who insisted that he was simply a common man and didn't want the job of king. She found that kind of thinking hypocritical. Much better to admit to enjoying the power and wealth that came with his station. After all, there were plenty of drawbacks to his position. Besides living in the proverbial fishbowl, his every movement and public utterance reported by journalists, he was surrounded by people currying favor, which made it difficult to tell friend from sycophant, never mind coups and assassination attempts and bottom feeders.

She had to admit that the man seemed comfortable in his own tanned and appealingly weathered skin. Did he fret over the fact that the assassin who killed his father hadn't been caught? How seriously did he take his position? Did he have doubts about the coronation ceremony which would ensure him of the rank of king for a lifetime? In Vashmira, the heir to the throne was given a year to try out the position of king and decide if he wanted to devote his life to ruling his people. That year was now almost over. According to Vashmiran law, before the coronation ceremony the heir must announce his intention to marry and name a bride. Afterward, he would rule until his death. She fully intended to ask him questions about his decision during their interview, but now was hardly the time, especially when he had yet to admit his identity to her.

As he steered the Mercedes from the airport, two powerful sedans holding his security team followed. Since he ignored them, she tried to do the same.

"Where do you wish to go?" Nicholas asked as if he'd set aside this time just to show her his country. She couldn't help being pleased. He was asking her what *she wanted* to see rather than taking her to what *he wanted* to show her.

"I'd like to take in Junar, your capital. I've heard the shops are quite fine."

"The lady wishes to shop?" She could hear no judgment in his tone, only a wary, withdrawn politeness, and wondered what he would do if she insisted on dragging him from store to store while she ogled trinkets and maxed out her credit cards—two things she hated doing.

"I need to evaluate the economic development in the downtown area for my story."

As his shoulders visibly relaxed, she suppressed a grin, suspecting he would have been appalled if she'd insisted on shopping. She couldn't picture him trailing her from store to store and carrying her purchases. He was too vital, too much a statesman for her to visualize him in such a capacity.

Perhaps the look in his eyes wasn't as interested or as personal as she'd thought. To test the notion, she crossed her legs and her skirt rode up exactly one inch above her knee. Not exactly scandalous behavior.

He looked. Discreetly.

She considered her position, wondering if she should go back to the airport and fly out of here. But it had only been a tiny glance, and he showed more self-control as he pulled smoothly into traffic on a modern two-lane highway. "What does evaluation of the downtown area mean?"

She rocked her foot slightly. A little less nervous now, she hoped he would keep his eyes on the busy road. "Stores, their merchandise and their customers can tell me a lot about a country's economy."

He grinned, a dazzling grin of challenge that told her that while she might want to keep their talk impersonal, he wouldn't stand for it. "You sure you don't just want to shop?"

She thought she could get used to his teasing. She wasn't all about work, although she could be when necessary. However much she sensed that this was one of those rare times where work and pleasure could overlap if she allowed it, she wouldn't. "I have a taste for the finer things in life, so I often find a way to work and enjoy myself at the same time."

"Efficient. I admire that."

His second glance at the hem of her skirt told her that her efficiency was not all he was admiring. He'd noticed her on a personal level, and she couldn't help being pleased by his reaction before she told herself her feelings were totally inappropriate. She'd chosen her clothes this morning with care. The neat navy jacket, white blouse and navy skirt were businesslike, prim and efficient, if one didn't count her silk hose and the high-heeled shoes she preferred that increased her height a good two inches, though she still barely came up to his chin.

"Tell me about your country," she requested.

His voice mellowed as he warmed to the subject. "This region of the world had always been a hotbed of political and religious insurrections going back to the eighth century and the Ottoman Empire. Problems continued into the late 1980s when the Iron Curtain fell and twenty satellite states declared their independence."

"That's when Vashmira declared independence?"

"Yes. For seventeen years, King Zared I guided Vashmira through astounding economic and political transformations." His tone revealed the pride he had in his father's accomplishments.

"The decades of the previous communist regime must have left scars," she prodded, curious to see if he would deny it.

"Not only on the economy and architecture, but also on the souls of our people."

"What do you mean?"

"A bottle of vodka can still buy a bribe from government officials. People in the tourist industry must be trained to smile. Gypsies fail to send their children to school. Better health care, higher education and a stable currency are objectives yet to be attained. And the military must still use a major part of their budget to guard Vashmira's many borders.''

She wanted to take out a notepad but refrained. Past experience told her that people spoke more freely without the visual reminders that their words might show up in print.

Nicholas drove into a city with wide boulevards and many parks. Buildings that looked as if they'd stood for centuries lent an old-world charm while the hustle and bustle of buses, hurrying pedestrians and tourists made the city look like a prosperous economic center. She noted a contrast of cultures, men in western business suits, Arabs in traditional robes, Jews wearing yarmulkes and two old Russian women wearing babushkas. The women were selling trinkets on the corner of a stone church with magnificent stained-glass windows that looked as if the crusaders had built it.

''Do you have open-market bazaars?'' she asked.

He glanced at her, looking both amused and surprised. ''On the weekends the farmers bring their fresh produce in from the villages to market.''

''Vashmira has its own currency and the value seems to be holding.''

''Yes, and dollars are just as acceptable as Vashmiran money.'' He spoke in a serious tone, his voice rich and dark like fine whiskey. ''We have our own stock market and a stable currency and hope to accept Euro dollars soon.''

She peeked over her shoulder at the two cars full of royal guards. ''I think someone's following us.''

"Really?" He sounded so innocent, but his eyes sparkled with amusement.

She pressed him harder to admit his true identity. "You're amazingly knowledgeable for a...driver."

He pulled over and parked, making his own spot in a tow-away zone. He had the grace to appear just a hint sheepish, yet still commanding and much too handsome. "You recognized me right away, didn't you?"

"I'm afraid I did. Would you mind explaining the reason for the ruse?"

"It was kind of you to go along, as my people are doing." He gestured to a park filled with laughing children, barking dogs, tourists and Muslims answering the call to prayer. "How about a stroll, some lunch and then a drive to a village?"

"Sure." While the seat of the car gave her plenty of room, she had a yen to escape the intimate quarters. No matter how much she tried to forget that she had a marriage contract with this man—she couldn't.

She'd travelled widely, but rarely had she met a man as quietly complicated as this one. He'd admitted to his deception with no explanation, only gentle evasion, and she suspected he would say nothing more if she didn't prod him for an answer.

He opened her door for her and she stood, refraining from stretching like a lazy cat. "Were you hoping I'd say I thought the king was an idiot?" she teased.

"Certainly not." He feigned indignation, then chuckled, a merry laugh that she wanted to hear more often. "I suppose my ruse seems odd to you."

"No odder than other customs." They headed away

from the street and into the park's center, and she thought she was handling the small talk quite well. If she directed the topic of conversation away from the personal, their relationship could remain professional. Eventually he'd feel comfortable enough with her to answer her questions about the difficulties of being a head of state. "I've covered stories about Tibet's holy men when they find a reincarnated soul. I've stayed in castles where intelligent people tell me there are ghosts. And I've been in countries where it's considered risqué for a woman to show her ankles."

"It must have been very difficult for you, since you have such lovely ones," he complimented her.

Damn! She'd stepped right into that one and barely refrained from wincing. That he didn't mind *revealing* that he'd noticed struck her as way too personal, but she cautioned herself that his statement didn't necessarily mean he wanted to hit on her. Some men offered compliments as easily as others opened a door for a woman.

"Thank you. Now tell me why your people pretend they don't recognize you," she said, again bringing their talk back to a more neutral topic.

The look he arrowed at her from the corner of his eye told her he understood what she was doing. Still, he responded with courtly courtesy. "The answer is really simple. Being a king is hard work. Sometimes I need a break."

His genuine response appealed to her on a basic level, but she restrained her feet from skipping along the sidewalk. This man's smooth European manners combined with an honesty that was rare in a head of state kept breaching the walls she'd built to keep the conversation and her emotions impersonal.

They headed into gardens of soaring sculptured hedges and intimate curving paths. "So what do you like to do when you're pretending not to be king?"

He eyed her with more than feigned suspicion. "Is this on the record?"

"Nick," her eyes challenged him, "with me, everything is on the record."

NICHOLAS COULDN'T WAIT to see his brother Alexander's face when he got a look at Ericka Allen, especially when he recalled his brother's comment that maybe she wouldn't be ugly. Her shoulder-length curly auburn hair, fair skin and green eyes were drawing more glances than he was. She was knock-your-boots-off gorgeous. Her fabulous hair sparkled in the sunlight. She had straight white teeth and full lips that were made for kissing. And her legs! Her legs made his mouth water. Those heels set her legs off to such advantage he had trouble not thinking of them wrapped around...

But it wasn't just her looks that had him thinking his father might have made a fine bargain after all. She was the complete package, beauty, brains and bravura all wrapped up into one alluring woman.

He admired her boldness and her businesslike attitude that was both pragmatic and adaptable. He suspected she and his sister Tashya would hit it off, but he was not eager to share her yet. Having her to himself was proving a delightful morning's diversion, certainly much more interesting than the budget analysis meeting with his finance minister that he'd skipped or the briefing with his secretary of state.

Instead of the refreshing Miss Allen, he'd expected a hard-nosed reporter who would pester him with questions he preferred not to answer. However, she was busy soaking in the atmosphere of the city, smiling at the kids flying kites, sniffing appreciatively at the rich aroma of Turkish coffee from a street vendor.

She was obviously a woman who enjoyed life, one who knew her own mind. She could exchange a glance of amusement with him, but there was nothing coy about her demeanor. Bold, direct and very American were adjectives that fit her. Despite the heels, she set a quick pace that most Vashmiran women would have found hurried. Her eager questions indicated a genuine interest in his people, and he wondered what she would write about his country. About him.

He'd noticed that she didn't like personal comments. Very professional, she let him know she was all business, yet she still managed to remain friendly. He suspected he would enjoy watching her work, but he would most especially enjoy the challenge of making her disregard that professionalism. Yet, he had to take care. He was not just any man pursuing any woman.

Her words could prove critical to the future of Vashmira. Stories about their multicultured country and recently stable economy would help their tourist industry. Just a short plane ride from Istanbul, Vashmira was well situated to attract more sightseers. However, if she emphasized their proximity to the troubled states of the former Soviet Union or to the volatile Middle

East, she could scare away not only tourists but companies who might otherwise invest in their growing satellite industry.

Ericka wandered toward one of Junar's more famous fountains, built during Stalin's era, and his security team followed. Since King Zared's assassination, no one in the royal family ventured out without protection. The ongoing murder investigations had come to many dead ends, and at this late date, Nicholas had little hope of ever seeing justice done. He worried that others in the royal family might become targets of an assassin still at large.

But there had been no other trouble since that fateful day. Not even a whiff of danger. The guards had caught no one attempting to sneak into the palace or trying to break through a crowd. There hadn't been so much as a threatening letter. Neither, however, had there been any such warning before his father's murder. Constant vigilance wore on Nicholas' nerves.

The ever-present security precautions had become an irritation. Now, however, the royal guards, apparently sensitive to Nicholas' wishes, fanned out, allowing Ericka and him the illusion of privacy.

The fountain's centerpiece consisted of a spectacular, massive stone sculpture of a soldier and his rearing warhorse, the animal's face a mask of terror, the soldier's triumphant.

He expected her to ask about the statue's history. But she brought up the topic he would have liked to avoid. "Have there been any new developments in the search for your father's assassin?"

Her inquiry came out of the blue, soft and sinuous.

She'd swept right to the hard question, and he suspected that she was interested in his reaction as much as his answer. The subject still pained him, he supposed it always would, but he could speak of the loss now without a lump in his throat.

That his father's and his last words had been argumentative still filled him with sadness. His father had been a loving man and well-loved in return. Nicholas would miss not only their spirited debates, but his wise advice, his honest humor and his example of how to rule sagely. But most of all, he would miss his infectious laughter.

The responsibility for attaining justice now rested on Nicholas. With the Ukraine to the north, Moldova, Romania and Bulgaria to the east and Turkey to the south, Vashmira was located at the point where Europe and Asia swirled together in a kaleidoscope of conflict, an area rife with enemies in the guise of neighbors—any one of which might have targeted his father. Finding the assassin had proven much more difficult than he'd hoped, but justice would be done.

King Zared had been a loving father, a great soldier, a crafty politician, and he owned the hearts of his people. The ''Hero of the Revolution's'' legacy must live on.

To ensure that his father's legacy continued, Nicholas had had to curb outward signs of his grief and assume the leadership role his father had prepared him for. He hadn't felt ready to accept the vast responsibilities or the weighty burden so suddenly thrust upon him, but he'd had no choice. The past year had been the toughest of his life, but he'd held Vashmira together.

And while marrying a woman for political reasons sat no better in his gut now than it had while his father still lived, the political necessity was greater. Required to announce his engagement before the coronation ceremony, he was truly snared by his father's wishes and the old marriage contract. He still could refuse to abide by it, but his father was so beloved by the Vashmiran people that if Nicholas balked without good reason, his people might refuse to follow his leadership. With his father gone forever, it was now up to Nicholas to keep the different factions from dividing his country. He couldn't risk a civil war—not even to pursue personal happiness.

Besides, even if he refused to marry the American, he had no one else to take her place. No one dear to his heart. Maybe his father's choice was for the best. His advisors expected him to make a political alliance, and his marriage to the American would strengthen badly needed ties to the West. His people had mourned their fallen leader, indeed would never forget him, but they also needed hope for the future. A royal marriage could give Vashmira a sense of stability, a chance for his father's legacy to continue.

Naturally, Ericka Allen would have her own opinions about a union between them. Odd, how she had never contacted him once in the decade since her eighteenth birthday when his father had notified her of the marriage contract. Hadn't she at least been curious? Obviously, she was no more keen on fulfilling their fathers' wishes than he, but was that admirable or not? On the one hand, he preferred a woman capable of independent thinking, one who didn't believe that becoming a queen meant a free ride and riches. On the other hand, a malleable wife would make his life easier—and Ericka Allen clearly had a mind of her own. Grave doubts over the wisdom of marrying a stranger was the reason he'd delayed meeting the American. However, now that she was here, he would try to persuade her to marry him.

Long before she'd arrived, he'd decided honesty was the best policy. After all, if his courtship succeeded, she might soon be his wife and part of the family. So he would have to discuss difficult subjects such as losing his father with her. But he'd console himself by drawing nearer to his inquisitor, breathing in her scent.

He leaned close enough to take in the lemony aroma of her freshly washed hair. "We suspect the assassination was accomplished from within the palace."

"An inside job?" She stepped toward the fountain, putting a little distance between them. "I thought he was shot through a window, from a distance."

He edged next to her again, but was careful not to touch her. "That's the story my press secretary released."

This time she held her ground, didn't inch away. "I am the press."

Hopefully not for too much longer. He had just a week to change her mind. "Our forensics people tell me the shooter was within five feet of my father, who was awake. Since he didn't shout for his guards, he either knew the man…"

''Or never saw him,'' she finished, her eyes large green pools of sympathy. ''Does it bother you to speak about his death?''

He kept his tone low, using the murmur of the water to wash over his words and keep them private. ''The pain is always in my heart. Whether I speak of him or not, the loss remains. My father was a wonderful man.''

She reached for his hand and squeezed, another gesture of compassion. ''I was sorry to learn of his death.''

Her hand was warm, her flesh soft, causing his heartbeat to accelerate. From her voice he could tell that she spoke not from courtesy, but from her true feelings, and he knew he was reacting inappropriately. And she was so lovely when she looked at him with such genuine sympathy.

But apparently she didn't avoid sad subjects anymore than she did difficult ones. ''Taking over the reins of the country must have been hard for you during a time of grief and uncertainty.'' She tugged to take her hand back, but he pretended not to notice, instead, lacing his fingers through hers.

''On the contrary, having so much work to keep me busy helped hold the grief at bay. Carrying on what my father started makes me feel closer to him.''

''I know what it's like to lose a parent.''

He kept her hand in his. ''King Zared told me your father was a courageous man.''

''I was thinking of my mother.'' Her voice grew fierce. ''She died from cancer the year after I graduated from college.''

She was all alone. He'd known that after reading her file but had forgotten. Now the details came back to him. She had no aunts or uncles, no siblings, no grandparents. He considered it helpful to his goal of keeping her in his country that she had no strong ties to leave behind.

"That's when I decided I wanted to be independently wealthy," she added with an urgency that surprised him.

Many people sought wealth, but most didn't declare their intentions so boldly. Her statement took him aback a little, but her honesty had him wanting to find out more. There were intriguing depths to this woman that he wanted to discover, a reaction far from usual.

"I don't understand." He didn't comprehend the connection between wealth and her mother's cancer, but the sharp determination in her tone, not greed, and a combination of anger and sorrow heightened his curiosity.

"Her insurance wouldn't cover a bone marrow transplant. They claimed the procedure was experimental. Accountants, not doctors, made the ultimate decision for my mother. It was cheaper for them to let her die."

"I'm sorry." He ran a hand through his hair, then gestured to a bench beside the fountain. "Such choices are always difficult. We're trying to raise standards of medical care here, as well. Technology, equipment, medicine and doctors are expensive."

"You have socialized medicine in Vashmira, don't you?" She sat beside him, her demeanor thoughtful, as if she was accustomed to keeping her emotions separate from her questions. She still allowed him to keep her hand, so that they sat close, thighs almost touching.

"Those who can pay, do so. We have free clinics for those who cannot, but it's an imperfect system. Those who are wealthy receive better health care than those who are poor. It's a system I would like to correct, but educating our children must come first."

"Why?" she asked, her tone nonconfrontational and curious, and he imagined her taking mental notes for her story. He supposed Alexander would be flirting boldly with her by now, but that was not Nicholas' way.

"To pay for better health care, we need a stronger economy. And to make our economy stronger, we need educated workers."

"It sounds so simple when you say it like that." She swayed toward him, then as if she thought better of it, rigidly straightened her spine.

"My father was first a student of business, then a soldier, then a king. He always told me to look past the numbers and use common sense."

"We could use more of that in my country," she admitted and he couldn't help respecting her for not holding the American government's system up to him as the idcal one. She seemed to understand there were strengths and weaknesses in every kind of government.

He wondered what her weakness was. She seemed so strong, so sure of herself. So independent. She sat on the bench without fidgeting, her shoulders square, her eyes alert. She'd crossed one leg over the other and her foot bounced up and down, the only sign she might not be as relaxed as she appeared.

Many women clammed up on him because of his position. Others flirted outrageously or put on airs. It was clear to him that Ericka Allen knew who she was, what she wanted and how to achieve her goals. An impressive woman with walls so high that he might never be able to break them down—not unless she herself invited him through a door.

She opened her purse and plucked out a coin. With a flick of her wrist, she tossed it into the fountain. "For luck."

He wanted to make her smile. "I believe you are a woman capable of making your own luck."

She smiled but it faded much too quickly. Tires squealed, and her eyes opened wide with alarm as a dark sedan jumped the curb and veered toward the fountain. Mothers screamed for their children. Several Arabs fled, one losing a sandal. The old Russian women drifted on, seemingly oblivious to the danger.

Nicholas' guards fired several shots at the car but failed to halt its progress as it continued to aim straight for the bench where they rested. There was no time to run far. No place to hide.

His security guards' bullets failed to stop the wildly careening car. Dark tinted windows prevented him from seeing the driver. However, from the speed and angle, he suspected a professional behind the wheel.

With only seconds to act, he found himself on his feet, Ericka's hand still firmly in his. As if of one mind, one thought, together they jumped into the fountain.

Chapter Three

Hand in hand, Nicholas and Ericka scrambled through the thigh-high fountain water toward the relative safety of the statue's massive base, putting several hundred tons of rock between the out-of-control car and the fragile skin and bone of their bodies. Together they rushed for cover behind the stone, and every time his guards fired a shot, Nicholas felt her hand flinch in his, but no sound passed her lips.

Soaked, weighed down by their clothes, they stumbled together, slipping and sliding. He steadied her once. A few steps later, he lost his footing, and with surprising strength, she yanked him up and toward the relative safety of the sculpture's base.

His guards fired relentlessly, shots pinged off the oncoming car. People in the park raced in panic for safety, many screaming. Animals sensed the danger, dogs barking and tugging on their leashes, and birds springing aloft in sudden flight. In the distance, a siren wailed. And on the streets surrounding the park, onlookers gawked, almost frozen in shock.

Just as fast as the danger began, it suddenly ended

with the car veering from the fountain and out of the park to drive with reckless abandon down a side street. Bystanders rushed to get out of the way. The Russian women's cart overturned, their wares scattering, and they shouted Russian obscenities at the dark sedan as it smashed into trash cans and flew around a corner to vanish from sight. One of security's dark sedans followed.

Ericka's soaking clothes stuck to her like a swimsuit, outlining her lean curves, accentuating her long legs, but this was no time to admire her slender body, Nicholas thought. She stood shivering from the frigid water, paying no heed to her condition, but surveying the action around her.

Another woman might have been trembling in fright, quaking at the close call with death or flinging herself into his arms to be soothed and comforted. He almost wished she'd chosen the latter. Instead, ever vigilant, Ericka courageously peeked between the horse's marble legs, calmly evaluating her surroundings. Her proficiency in assessing danger without showing her emotions must come in handy in her career. That particular trait was also indispensable for a soldier.

Or a queen.

His guards plunged through the fountain, taking positions around them, shielding their bodies like the Secret Service did the U.S. president. Their dramatics were for nothing. The car was long gone.

"What if your guards lose sight of him?" she asked.

He still stayed close to her, just in case trouble returned and they had to dash around the fountain. "They have radioed to alert the police."

"By the time the police join the chase, that driver will have ditched the car, which is probably stolen, and they'll have wiped clean the prints."

That her mind worked so logically and coolly under pressure both fascinated and amazed him. "You sound like a police officer."

"I once covered the paper's police beat," she explained with a bit of impatience.

How could she remain so professional while she stood so close to him that he could feel her every shiver? Didn't she want a hug, some human contact after almost losing her life? However, if she could remain so detached, he was not about to act otherwise. "That driver may not be working alone."

His suggestion had her pausing, thinking, her head cocking at an angle. "You think it's a conspiracy?"

"I didn't say that. My guards' first priority is not to catch the driver, but to protect *us*."

"Like they could stop a speeding vehicle with those little guns?"

"Would you feel better if my men carried bigger guns?" he asked, somewhat amused by her attitude now that he was relatively sure the danger had passed and that no one had been hurt.

"I'd feel better if you caught the guy who just tried to make roadkill out of us."

"Roadkill?"

"Sorry, it's an American idiom. Your English is so good I forget it's not your native language."

"Four years at Princeton didn't familiarize me with the term 'roadkill.'"

"It means 'dead meat.'"

He couldn't believe they were having this semantics discussion in the middle of a fountain while she stood there shivering. Her lips were a dark blue, but he'd wager they could turn purple and she still wouldn't come close enough to him to share body heat. Just what he needed, another challenge. But after all, he had nothing else to do. The investigation into his father's murder and his meetings with his finance minister and secretary of state would just have to be put on hold while he convinced this woman she wanted to marry him, he thought sarcastically. He immediately realized that she was already affecting the way he thought—he was rarely sarcastic.

"Your Highness." Ira Hanuck, his chief security guard came up beside them, ignoring the slosh of water. Gangly, raw-boned and Slavic, Ira's wolflike expression looked fierce enough to stop an enemy in his tracks. "I've ordered a guard to bring up your car. We should return to the safety of the palace."

"I'd say a change of clothes is in order," Nicholas agreed. Throughout the entire exchange, he'd kept hold of Ericka's hand. At least she'd allowed him that much, although she probably couldn't think of a polite way to extract it. To him, touching her seemed natural and easy as they splashed back the way they'd come toward his car. Although he told himself not to make too much of her acceptance of his hand, he couldn't help but feel pleased that she didn't attempt to pull away now that the danger had passed.

His guard drove the car over the park's sidewalks, directly toward them. The crowds had long ago scattered, and only a few curious onlookers had returned. His vigilant men surrounded them, but when one of them opened the rear door for her, Ericka halted, hesitating to enter the vehicle.

He wondered if she feared being with him or a car bomb or something else he hadn't thought of. She had no way of knowing that his men never left his car unguarded on a city street, or that it was bulletproof—an expensive but necessary precaution after his father's death.

With her hair damp, spikes of water on her lashes and her wet clothes, she should have looked like a vulnerable, half-drowned cat, but she was fresh, clean and appealing. She tried and failed to pluck her wet blouse and jacket from her skin, but the weight of the water in the fabric plastered the material against her. ''Our wet clothes will ruin your beautiful leather seats.''

He marvelled that she worried over his car, not her own safety. ''Ira, isn't there a blanket in the trunk?''

Within moments his men had retrieved the blanket. Ericka's teeth chattered, and her lips were almost as blue as her ruined suit. Even her ankles looked blue. Nicholas wrapped the blanket around her, helped her into the car, and took the seat beside her, then ordered the driver. ''Turn the heat on full.''

When Ericka's teeth continued to chatter, he lifted her onto his lap, unable to resist taking her into his arms.

''I-I'm f-f-fine,'' she protested.

"No, you are not. I am accustomed to swimming in cold water but you are almost frozen."

Hoping to warm her with his own body heat, he nonetheless expected her to protest again, but it was a measure of how thoroughly cold she really was that she said nothing.

"Better?" he asked.

Even through the thick blanket, he could feel her shivering. "Much better. That water was cold. And you are…" she almost, but not quite fluttered her eyelashes, "very warm."

He was warm all right and with her sitting so close, he was about to get much warmer. But he said nothing about the direction his thoughts kept taking. He should be concerned with her security, her safety, not the lush curve of her bottom against his thighs or the heat of her minty breath against his neck.

The driver headed out of the park. Security teams escorted them, front and back. "Sir, we shouldn't take the most direct route back to the palace."

"I'm well aware of procedure." The trip would take longer than usual, but Nicholas didn't mind. Considering the pleasant bundle in his arms, he didn't mind at all. "Do the best you can."

"Yes, Your Highness."

During the danger, Ericka had kept a cool head, even helping him after he'd slipped on the slick bottom of the fountain. She hadn't once screamed, hadn't complained afterward that he'd failed to protect her. She'd really remained surprisingly calm, and while he marvelled at her composure in perilous circumstances, he wondered how many other dangerous situations she'd been in and what she'd written about them. Was she the kind of woman to save her complaints for her story?

He looked down into a face that appeared innocent of that kind of duplicity and had to remind himself she had a mind as sharp as his secretary of state's. From the tilt of her head and the concentration on her face, he suspected she was working out details for her story.

"Could the driver of that car have been drunk?" she asked him.

He almost smiled at her question. Only Ericka Allen could talk business while she sat on his lap. "Anything's possible. Why?" He hoped she didn't intend to write a story about the incident, play it up and make it seem more dangerous that it had been. He could minimize the coverage here, and normally no foreign countries picked up Vashmira's national news. His country simply wasn't important enough to warrant that kind of worldwide interest.

"Well, at first I thought the driver was aiming at us…"

He'd thought so too. His guards had cleared people away from the bench and fountain to give him a measure of privacy and protection. He and Ericka had been the only people directly in the car's path. "But?"

"At the last minute, the driver spun the wheel and shot away. If he intended to run us over, why not drive right into the fountain after us?"

"Because if he drove in, he *couldn't* have driven out?" Nicholas suggested, thinking he could hold her like this for hours, enjoying the fresh scent of her damp hair, gazing into her lovely green eyes, which were focusing on him with concentration.

She leaned her head back against his shoulder, showing him the arch of a delectable-looking neck. "You think he didn't want to get caught?"

"Would you?"

"Maybe he wasn't after you. Maybe it was an accident. A drunk driver lost control of the car, then fear scared him sober enough to yank on the wheel, avoid us and the fountain."

"It's possible," he murmured, his breath close enough to mix with hers.

"But you don't think so?"

He considered lying to her so she wouldn't write about this incident, but instinct stopped him. "The driver looked like a professional to me, but I'd prefer you didn't write that in your story."

"If he was a pro, would he have missed?" she asked, totally ignoring his request.

For the first time he realized the danger he faced— not only from a potential assassin but from the sexy bundle in his arms who'd already told him everything was on the record. She had a casual manner of questioning him that made him think of her as a friend, as a woman, not a respected correspondent who had the power to cause trouble within Vashmira's borders if she wrote an unfavorable story.

"No one could have predicted we'd stop in that park," she muttered, thinking it through. "Maybe we were followed from the airport."

While he wanted to answer her questions honestly, she was in a position to use his answers against him, compromise security and incite civil unrest. Although her story would be published overseas, Vashmiran newspapers and television stations would report back here on what she wrote. He already had enough problems; he didn't need more.

Perhaps he should have lied and told her that he believed the driver had been drunk. But what kind of way was that to start a relationship? He'd preferred honesty and realized he'd put himself in an extremely awkward position. He risked damaging their potential relationship if he stretched the truth, but risked compromising security if he didn't.

"Your Majesty," the driver glanced at him in the rearview mirror. "There are protesters blocking our route to the palace."

"What kind of protest?" Ericka asked, squirming to one side and moving off his lap.

Nicholas took care of business and spoke first to the driver. "Can we go around?"

The driver pressed his hand to his earpiece, a tiny radio device through which he received orders. "The chief suggests we head for Montene until the streets calm."

"Do it. Are the protests violent?" Nicholas asked, then could have bit his tongue. He was accustomed to guarding his words when he spoke to the press, but not in private. He didn't want Ericka to think she was in danger, write about his country as if today's incident was an everyday occurrence and scare away tourists over a minor affair.

"Sorry, Your Highness. I have no further information and the radio won't work on this side of the ridge.''

''Understood.'' Nicholas leaned back in the seat, took one look at Ericka's arched eyebrow and selected his next words with care. ''We aren't in danger.''

''Of course not. Your guards were just shooting at that car in the park for target practice. No doubt your protesters are marching to burn off calories.''

He almost smiled at her wit. ''You Americans love your sarcasm.''

''We also love the truth,'' she countered.

Soft and silky and sensuous, she peered into his eyes with an acute intelligence that challenged him to explain. He dropped his gaze to her straight nose and full lips, wondered if she'd taste as good as she looked. Although she'd scooted off his lap, they sat close together, so close that he need merely dip his head to capture her lips.

She must have read his intentions. A cocky tilt of her eyebrow, a slight increase in the dilation of her pupils and a ragged breath told him she was respond-ing to him, but clearly didn't like it.

She must be accustomed to men taking her into their arms, trying to kiss her. He wanted to be different from the rest. Waiting until she was receptive would be the wisest move. However, pulling back wasn't easy, and he had to remind himself that he plotted not just a seduction, but a courtship.

''The truth,'' he told her, ''is that on any given day, someone in this country is angry at me. We always have protesters in our streets. These particular pro-testers want to open our northern borders to accept more immigrants. But the majority of Vashmiran people are against such a move. We simply cannot afford the financial burden of caring for additional refugees.''

As he spoke, he studied her carefully and realized that she'd accepted his decision not to kiss her with just a mere flicker of relief. Superb at hiding her feelings, she could respond on many levels without batting an eyelash. Yet, when he'd pulled back, for just an instant, he'd seen surprise and possibly disappointment battle with relief.

''Since you weren't elected, how do you know what the majority of people want?'' she challenged him again.

''We have meetings and take polls here, too. We are not so backward.''

''I didn't mean to imply that you were. I'm not sure anyone in government really understands working folks.''

''It's not so hard to listen to people.… We all basically have the same wants and needs.''

''We do?'' The concept appeared to interest her.

''Yes, I believe so. We all want to live in a safe neighborhood, have enough food on our table, educate our children, heal our sick, care for the elderly. And let's not forget our need for the freedom to pursue happiness and fall in love.''

At the word *love,* a stillness came over her. She appeared to concentrate so completely that he felt as if she'd gone somewhere else. When a full minute passed and she said nothing, he waved a hand in front of her eyes. ''Ericka. Ericka. Where are you?''

"Sorry." She squirmed to put inches between them on the seat.

He could only be thankful for the patience his father had demanded he learn as a child because he ached to draw her back against his side—even though he knew he would be moving too fast for her. So he controlled himself—barely. "Where did you go off to in your head?"

"I was just thinking…" She bit her bottom lip.

Was she deliberately teasing him? He doubted she even realized the effect she was having on him. "Thinking about what?"

"You think every human being needs love?" she asked him, her eyes honest, but wary.

"Absolutely."

She grinned. "No hesitation. No equivocation. I like that."

"And you disagree?"

"It depends on the definition of need," she told him. "I need air, food and water or I'd die. However, without love, I certainly wouldn't die."

"But would you be happy?" he pressed, a little puzzled by the turn the conversation had taken. The woman on the seat beside him was beautiful, smart and full of startling revelations, so much so that he found himself holding his breath as he waited for her to reply.

"I am happy," she told him. "My life is very much the way I planned it."

"You have no husband? No children? And nothing's missing?"

"If I had those kind of permanent ties," she countered, "I wouldn't be here with you. And right now, I can't think of a better place to be."

When she leaned toward him and looked at him with intensity, those eyes peering straight into him, he had difficulty thinking, breathing. He leaned down, kissed her forehead. "I'm glad you came."

"MONTENE IS OUR SUMMER beach house on the Black Sea," Nicholas told Ericka twenty minutes later. "We can stay there until the protesters get hungry and tired and go home."

She looked out the window at the very blue water. Sailboats, the occasional sailboarder and swimmers took advantage of the temperate climate and calm waters, which matched those of any European resort along the Mediterranean. Sunbathers reclined on lounge chairs around swimming pools or lay on colorful towels spread on the golden sand beach. Along the roadside, a Turkish mosque reminded her that Vashmira had one foot firmly in the East.

The driver's route wound around a grassy hill, and she lost sight of the sparkling water and contented herself with viewing the magnificent Mediterranean villas in the area. Both rustic and magnificent homes of varying architectures dotted the landscape. As they approached the seashore, early nineteenth-century homes characterized by stone ground floors and wooden upper floors gave way to ornate homes built more recently that sported sunny verandas, multicolored facades and jutting eaves. Colorful and welcoming wildflowers sprouted in window boxes, planters and along the sidewalks. Ivy-covered perimeter fences or massive hedges and thick gates hid the summer homes of Vashmira's wealthy. Clearly this was an area where the owners valued their privacy, and Ericka could easily enjoy vacationing here, but she reminded herself this was not a vacation. She had work to do and turned her attention from the view to her host.

"You're looking forward to staying a while?" she asked, breathing in the scent of flowers through the now open window, at the same time trying to forget how good it had felt when he'd wrapped his arms around her. She'd absorbed the warmth of his body, and she no longer needed his arms around her—but she wanted them. However, she absolutely wouldn't make a move in his direction. She never flirted with the men she interviewed. Her job required a clear head, and she refused to let personal feelings interfere with her career. Long ago she had set limits, limits that didn't include mixing business and pleasure, since she wouldn't consider tarnishing her professional reputation. Which didn't mean she didn't like men—just that she kept that area of her life separate from work. Unfortunately, work often kept her on the road for weeks, not exactly conducive to maintaining a relationship. While she had no interest in Nicholas beyond obtaining a terrific interview, she still couldn't help recalling how hard it had been to force herself to scoot away.

It wasn't as if she'd never sat on a man's lap before. But she'd never before felt so aware. She'd noticed every rise and fall of his chest as he'd breathed, heard his steady heartbeat under her cheek, but worst of all, she'd never felt so attracted to a man. However, she could handle it. Many famous people had charisma. That didn't mean her relationship would be anything but professional.

"I am looking forward to a break from state business. There's no finance minister, secretary of state or military advisor waiting for me here. No tedious meetings. No protesters."

He sounded boyishly happy, and she smiled in response. "So you're playing hooky with me, and you have a good excuse."

"Exactly."

Ericka liked the way he dealt with the protesters. No macho call to bring out the troops. No embarrassment over the fact that he couldn't return to the palace. No complaint over the inconvenience. Just a simple change of plans which he'd adapted to his benefit. And hers.

His calm, rational thinking gave her hope that he would not ever attempt to use that old marriage contract against her. He seemed thoroughly modern and at ease with himself.

Although she wasn't naive enough to think they would be alone in the summerhouse, their time together here would probably be less scheduled and more relaxed than at the palace. While she regretted that her baggage had been sent elsewhere, she had her laptop and could work.

However, she wasn't nearly ready to start writing. She still had much data to collect. In fact, she had yet to decide how to slant her first story. Her impressions of the king kept changing. When she'd asked about his father he'd been almost dark and brooding, minutes later he'd been cheerful and entertaining. While he was clearly a dedicated workaholic, she often caught hints of intriguing playfulness.

She'd give up a shot at this year's Pulitzer prize to know his intentions toward her. One moment she'd seen sparks of desire in his eyes and had thought he would kiss her, the next, he'd been remote, as if he'd had to pull himself back from a natural impulse and remind himself to go slowly.

She was woman of the world enough to know she was having an effect on him. But she also knew she wasn't sending him signals of encouragement. So why did she feel as if she were being subjected to a slow, methodical campaign to bring down her defenses? She considered and rejected the idea that he was deliberately trying to create such an impression. No doubt the man simply oozed charm 24/7 and couldn't help himself.

The tension between them wouldn't go on for too much longer without him at least trying to kiss her. Although she would avoid the situation if possible and had no intention of kissing him back, she couldn't help wondering if his kiss might be as seductive as the looks he gave her. Past experience told her that saying no to him might cause difficulties. Some men sulked when she refused their advances. Others refused to cooperate with the interview. But she could cope with this behavior as she had in the past.

She was dying to ask him who he intended to announce as his bride at the coronation ceremony but didn't yet dare. She didn't want him to clam up on her.

In some ways this assignment was turning out better than she'd expected. Nicholas Zared had surprised her and intrigued her. He would make a fascinating study for her story. Commanding, compelling, capable, he didn't try to throw his weight around.

Pavement turned to brick, and the driver drove through an impressive set of gates manned by two guards. Well acquainted with the lifestyles of the wealthy, she nonetheless marvelled at the luxury of the lush private grounds. Exotic greenery and a glorious variety of flowers surrounded gurgling fountains and an elaborate gazebo. A patrol discreetly monitored the perimeter, their leashed dogs sniffing towering hedges.

The driveway ended in a graceful circle in front of a sprawling stone beach house that looked as if the architect couldn't decide whether he was building a castle, a museum or a mosque. The crazy architecture, a patchwork quilt from various styles and eras, had a certain charm.

Ericka kept the blanket around her shoulders and stepped out of the car. The fresh scent of the sea wafted to her on the breeze along with the sweet aroma of flowers, and the shouts of happy children carried through the air from the beach. She wondered if security there was just as tight but was reluctant to bring up the topic and break the peaceful moment.

Nicholas carried her laptop for her, but instead of strolling toward the massive staircase leading to the front entrance, he headed for a side door. "I thought you might appreciate a hot bath and a change of clothes before you meet anyone."

"Thanks." The man could be considerate. As a woman who paid attention to her looks, she didn't like meeting people at such a disadvantage. With her damp hair, wet clothes and smeared makeup, she looked far from her best and would have felt uncomfortable meeting anyone new. Only Nicholas' similar appearance, his casual acceptance of their situation and genuine good manners kept her from worrying over her appearance with him. However, meeting strangers was another matter.

Nicholas led her down a private brick path and opened a gate which led into a courtyard shaded by huge trees and ivy-covered walls. Mosaic tiles decorated a patio area where Ericka had no trouble imagining spending a pleasant afternoon curled up with a political thriller. A marble chess set stood waiting for players, and chirping birds bathed in a fountain that spouted clear water into a pond with golden-colored fish.

"I could get used to this," she told him.

His eyes lit up. "Wait until you see the Turkish bath." He led her to a door of the main building. "An Ottoman emperor built the original baths and my father had them restored."

"Sounds interesting."

"There's a men's side and a ladies' side."

"And never the two shall mix?" she teased, then wished she could take back her words. Whether she liked it or not, sitting on his lap had made their relationship less formal.

"I didn't say that." As if she'd placed a naughty visual image in his mind, his lips curled into a tight grin, but he turned away before she could tell if his mouth blossomed into a full-fledged smile.

He took them up a spiral flight of stairs, then another. The lighting was dim, the stairs dusty. It wasn't hard to visualize former residents sneaking up and down this secret passageway to rendezvous with a lover.

"Here we are." Nicholas opened a door, and she followed him into a stunning room decorated in deep blues and golden hues. Fresh flowers in Venetian glass vases lent a sweet scent to the sea breeze coming in through open floor-to-ceiling windows that looked out onto a veranda, the beach and the sea. A domed ceiling overhead reminded her of the mosques she'd seen in Istanbul, but except for the plush Turkish carpets and Russian paintings on the walls, the decor was European. She recognized museum quality antiques in the furnishings, a crystal chandelier from the last century, priceless art on mahogany-paneled walls. Then she peeked into the most modern of bathrooms, all gleaming white marble, elegant golden faucets for the sink and tub, and her very own whirlpool, steam bath and sauna. She snared a towel and wrapped her wet hair into a turban.

A huge closet stood open, and her lower jaw dropped in amazement as she recognized her belongings. Her luggage had been delivered here and unpacked for her!

She whirled around to thank him, thinking a girl could get used to this kind of first-class treatment. "Thanks for having my stuff sent over. This is the loveliest room I've ever seen."

He set her laptop on a desk. "I'm pleased you like it."

"I'm so glad I came." She crossed over to him, the blanket still around her shoulders but wanting him to know how much his thoughtfulness meant to her. "I almost didn't accept the assignment, you know."

"Really? Why is that? I can't imagine that you were overwhelmed by being picked for the only personal interview."

"Not a chance of that happening." So he knew of her ambitions and had played upon them. Interesting. "And you knew it, didn't you?" she asked him, curious to see how he would respond since neither of them had yet mentioned the marriage contract between them. She'd thought, no hoped, that he'd forgotten its existence. But she now realized she'd been wrong.

"I arranged to offer you what you wanted," he admitted with no hesitation, his eyes direct and compelling.

"Why?"

"To get what I wanted," he admitted, his voice as sweet as spun sugar.

"Which is?" she pushed him, needing to know exactly what she had gotten herself into.

"I wanted the best journalist for the job."

"Bull."

His eyes narrowed. "I haven't lied to you."

"But you haven't told me the whole truth either, have you?" she countered, her temper starting to sizzle.

"I thought it was time we met," he admitted.

Before he could say another word, a woman burst

through the door which remained open from their entrance. For a moment, Ericka feared another attack.

Then she took a second look. Extremely attractive, with long dark hair, a killer figure and flashing eyes, the woman rushed toward Nicholas and flung herself into his arms with the exuberance of someone assured he would welcome her.

She kissed him on one cheek, then the other, then on the mouth. "Darling, I'm so glad you're all right."

Chapter Four

"We're fine." Nicholas turned to Ericka, who looked as if she couldn't decide whether to hide or flee or stay and meet his vibrant sister. She stayed.

With her cheeks pink, and a few dry wisps of hair peeking out from under the turban, Ericka looked less sophisticated, younger. Adorable. Shorter.

Shorter? Without her heels, she'd lost at least two inches of her height. Funny, how he thought of her as tall. She wasn't, not really. He estimated her height at about five feet five inches, yet she still gave the appearance of tallness and strength. It wasn't just her excellent posture that gave him that impression but her cool courage. The way she fearlessly met difficulties head on. He'd never forget that with bullets flying around her and a car bearing down on her, she hadn't cowered but coolly noted the details, peeking through the hooves of the statue.

Even now, he knew her sharp mind was noting details about Tashya. He was eager to read what she wrote about him, his people and his country and yet reluctant because he might be disappointed.

Quickly, he introduced the two women, curious to see their reactions to one another. "Ericka Allen, I'd like you to meet my sister, Princess Tashya Zared."

Ericka held out her hand.

"You're almost family." Tashya ignored the American's outstretched hand, kissed Ericka on both cheeks and then the mouth. Nicholas had to give Ericka credit. She adjusted as easily as a diplomat to the Eastern European greeting and without a change of expression.

Tashya, immaculately dressed in riding attire, took one look at Ericka's wet clothes and went into one of her typical tirades. "I heard you two went for a swim. Ericka, thank goodness you saved Nicholas when he slipped in that fountain or he might have drowned."

Ericka broke into an unguarded grin at Tashya's exaggeration, and he couldn't help wishing she'd smile so easily at him. "I would never allow the King of Vashmira to drown."

Nicholas could tell the women were going to hit it off famously. Although he was pleased, he just knew he would be a convenient target. Tashya, alone, was a handful. She and Ericka ganging up on him, to use an American idiom, might be dicey. "Ladies, I do know how to swim, and even if I didn't, the water was only up to our thighs."

Tashya shook her head at him as if he'd just spouted nonsense. "But you're wet up to your eyebrows, so your head went under. If she'd been weak and fainted, you would have stopped to carry her, which you would have no doubt enjoyed just as much as Alexander, although you would never admit it, especially—"

"Tashya." He tried to make his voice stern.

Ericka's grin widened, and she barely muffled a delighted chuckle.

"—since, she's so gorgeous—"

"Thank you," Ericka said, apparently quite pleased.

"—and even though you are strong, and she doesn't weigh any more than me, you would have slowed down if you'd had to carry her, and then that car might have struck you and—"

"Slow down. We're both fine, and somehow I don't think Ericka is the fainting type."

"Of course, she isn't. Didn't I just *say* that?" Tashya sighed, rolling her eyes dramatically. "But it's rude of you to keep her standing there in wet clothes when she could be in a hot bath, or the sauna or on the beach soaking up the sun. Brother, where are your manners?"

"They must have drowned in the fountain."

Tashya shrugged her elegant shoulders and spoke to Ericka as if he wasn't there. "He thinks he's funny, but he isn't. He also works too hard, but I think you will be good for him, yes?"

Ericka shook her head. "I don't know."

"You see why I tried to marry her off?" Nicholas complained to Ericka without bothering to hide his affection for Tashya. His sister might be spoiled, might wear her emotions where all could see them, but her heart was pure. "I found her a perfectly good Moldovan prince and—"

"He had the breath of a horse."

"She refused the man who would have made a fine ally for our country," Nicholas argued.

"His castle smelled like pond scum."

Nicholas shrugged. "My sister is a finicky woman."

"I'm particular, aren't you?" Tashya asked Ericka.

Ericka locked gazes with his sister, and they exchanged long knowing glances, clearly in complete agreement. Over what, he didn't have a clue.

Ericka nodded and her makeshift turban fell off. "I'm very particular."

Tashya fingered a wisp of Ericka's hair. "Oh, I adore that particular shade of red. It's rare in this part of the world."

"In my part of the world, too. However if you want to try it, I brought an extra bottle." Ericka admitted to dyeing her hair as easily as another woman might have to polishing her fingernails. Her openness surprised him. In his experience, for some reason, women seemed to want men to think they came by their looks naturally—a notion that made no sense to him. Ericka's honesty seemed like a breath of fresh sea air.

However, before Ericka talked Tashya into dyeing her beautiful black hair auburn, Nicholas grabbed his impetuous sister by the arm. "Let's allow my guest some privacy to take that shower."

"Right." Tashya looped her arm through Nicholas' arm, nodded goodbye and spoke to Ericka over her shoulder on their way out. "Lunch is served in half an hour on the back terrace. Perhaps afterward, we can all go riding."

His sister didn't even wait for the door to shut behind them before she skipped a little. "I like her,

Nicholas. She's got a sense of humor. She's not stuck up, and she has a brain.''

"How would you know? You didn't let her get a word in edgewise.''

"Yes, but I read her file.'' She squeezed his arm. "Did you know she interviewed Prince Charles? And Princesses Caroline and Stephanie? And Mel Gibson? I've read her stuff. She's good, insightful. Now, she and I are going to be sisters.''

"You're jumping to conclusions. We just met today.''

"It's going to work out, I just know it.''

"Really?'' It always amazed him that his sister could so blithely believe that what she wanted to happen would happen. "The woman is only interested in her story, not me.''

Tashya started to say something, but stopped, a rarity for her. She gave him an odd look that he couldn't read. "Then you'll just have to convince her otherwise, won't you? I've always wanted a sister. No offense to you and Alexander and our baby brothers, but it will be great to have another woman my age around here. Do you think she likes to ride? How about hiking? I could take her up into the village and—''

Accustomed to his sister's enthusiastic chatter, Nicholas let her talk. He understood she often felt alone. Their father had adored and spoiled Tashya, who had grown up accustomed to having her own way. When his father married Sophia, she had tried to rein in Tashya's stubborn exuberance—but with little success. His sister was much too adventuresome and too smart for the gentle Sophia to handle.

He feared he'd had less luck influencing his sister than their father. Maybe Ericka would be good for her. But with his luck, the two of them would mean double the trouble.

"Nicholas!"

"What?" They had reached his apartment, an entire wing in the summerhouse set aside for his use. Alexander and Tashya had their own apartments as did Sophia and the boys. His sister was looking at him impatiently as if he, too, wasn't entitled to a hot shower and a change of dry clothes. He hadn't been listening and wondered why Tashya's face had turned so serious.

"I met Ira on the way here. He said the car that almost ran you over was found shortly after, abandoned. He traced the plates, and the car was stolen. No fingerprints which means—"

"Nothing. Someone could have been out for a joyride, gotten scared and—"

She drilled him with a serious sisterly stare. "Nicholas, don't treat me as if I have no more brains than a dandelion. That car was driven by a trained assassin, and we both know it."

Sometimes with all her chatter, he forgot how smart his sister was. "I'm sorry. I didn't want you to worry."

"I'd worry less if we knew the identity of the car's driver."

Tashya's words sounded remarkably like those Ericka had said to him earlier. Although the two women looked nothing alike, although they came from different worlds, they both spoke with admirable conviction.

"What would you have me do?" he asked his sister.
"I can't exactly go into hiding and still run this country."

"Just promise me that you'll be cautious," Tashya
said.

Nicholas affectionately tugged a lock of her long,
dark hair. "Count on it."

ERICKA SHED HER WET clothes in the bathroom and
turned on the golden water tap for the shower. She
washed her hair, then plugged the drain. The luxurious
tub filled quickly, and she poured in a liberal dose of
bath crystals which bubbled invitingly and filled the
room with a cinnamon aroma. With a deep sigh of
satisfaction, she slid into the tub's hot water and under
the frothy bubbles until she was cocooned in warmth
up to her neck, closed her eyes and let the heat soothe
her.

After the close call in the park, Ericka's mind had
been filled with the possibility that she'd just witnessed another assassination attempt, so meeting Nicholas' sister had been a delightful distraction. She'd
liked Tashya at first sight, liked her exuberance, her
sense of humor, and her openness. And she sensed a
keen intelligence behind the woman's charming playfulness. The obvious love and affection between
brother and sister had been touching. Ericka had always known she'd missed a lot by being an only child.
Now that her mother was gone, she noticed the lack
more than usual. It would have been wonderful to have
someone with whom to share childhood memories.

This rare reflective mood wouldn't last long. Not

when the present offered so many interesting possibilities. Nicholas hadn't come right out and said the reason he'd invited her here was that he knew about their marriage contract, but he'd implied it. Although she thought him quite attractive, his agile mind sexy, she had no plans to stay in Vashmira. No intention of giving up her career or the life she'd worked so hard to achieve, even if she did sense a special awareness between them. She forced her tense muscles to relax in the warm bathwater, determined to continue to investigate and interview and write a series of articles, enjoy her stay here, leave, and remember the time fondly.

While she'd been in dangerous situations before, she hadn't expected to remain so tense afterward and wondered if her unease had more to do with her feelings about Nicholas than the danger. He's just a handsome man, she told herself. Relax. No one would disturb her since the palace security was first rate. She was safe.

"Is she dead?"

At the childlike voice, Ericka opened her eyes.

Oh God! She wasn't alone.

Sternly, she consoled herself with the thought that palace assassins didn't sneak around in the bodies of children. Two little boys stared at her. She slumped lower in the tub, crossed her arms over her breasts beneath the suds.

"She moved."

The oldest child couldn't be more than five, the other maybe three or a little younger. Dark-haired and dark-eyed, they stared at the mountain of foaming bubble bath that blanketed her completely. The taller child held the younger boy's hand, leaned forward and squinted at her.

What should she say?

"I'm taking a bath," Ericka explained the obvious, wondering where the duo came from and if they were Nicholas' much younger brothers. From her research she'd learned that after Nicholas, Alexander and Tashya's mother had died, King Zared I had married Sophia Varna, a native-born Vashmiran. Together they'd had three additional children, all boys. Unfortunately, Ericka's files held only baby pictures, and she couldn't be sure if these were the same children.

She smiled crookedly. "My name is Ericka Allen, can you tell me your names?"

"Dimitri."

"Kita."

So they *were* Nicholas' brothers. Although it was difficult to discern their features through their chubby baby faces, she detected the merest suggestion of Nicholas' strong chin.

"His real name is Nikita but he can't say it yet," Dimitri explained in unaccented English.

Nikita frowned at his brother but didn't let go of Dimitri's hand.

"Kita is a fine name," Ericka told him. "So is Dimitri. Do you boys live here?"

"Nope," Dimitri said.

Kita shook his head.

Now what? Ericka thought she had been doing so well. Although she hadn't been around children often, she didn't expect to feel so helpless. She imagined that someone was looking frantically for these little rascals, yet she didn't want to shoo them away unattended. They were too young to wander about alone. However, she couldn't reach the towel without revealing a lot of skin, and the bubbles covering her wouldn't last forever.

"Are you lost?" she asked.

"No. Are you?" Dimitri said. Nikita placed the thumb of his free hand into his mouth and sucked contentedly.

"I was invited here," Ericka explained as simply as she could. "Does your mother know where you are?"

At her question the two boys looked at one another and grinned. She might not be experienced with children, but their mischievous expressions revealed that these boys knew their mother was looking for them.

Dimitri turned back to Ericka. "Mother will find us."

Kita took his thumb out to add, "Always does."

"Ericka!" Nicholas' voice carried to her from the bedroom.

She was trapped naked in the bathtub by a toddler and a five-year-old kid, and Nicholas would soon rush through the door. Why did such embarrassing moments happen to her? She'd always been so organized, now she felt as if she'd climbed a tree and had swung out onto a shaky branch and her stomach trembled at the thought of a fall.

The kids might be adorable, but the bubbles in her bath were alarmingly low, the water cooling and Nicholas' footsteps fast approached.

Oh, God.

"Dimitri, could you hand me that towel, please?" she asked, then called out to Nicholas, "I'm in the bathroom. And I'm not alone. I've just made the acquaintance of two gentlemen by the names of Dimitri and Nikita. You wouldn't be looking for them by any chance, would you?"

Just as Dimitri pulled the towel off its warming rack, Nicholas stuck his head through the doorway. He took in the missing boys and her predicament in a glance and his lips twitched. "What are you two doing in here?"

"Handing Miss Ericka her towel."

Ericka whipped the towel from him, held it up like a shield and stood before wrapping it around her.

"I can see that." Admiration warmed his tone. She believed she was completely hidden, as she stood holding the towel in front of her, but she'd forgotten the damn mirror.

While Ericka's body was completely concealed from the boys' sight, Nicholas' gaze had seen her reflection. He must have gotten an eyeful of soapy flesh before she wrapped the thick terry cloth around herself, preserving her modesty if not restraining a blush.

Ericka had never been more appreciative of a giant-sized towel or felt so aware of her body. At the heat in Nicholas' eyes, her breasts tightened. Damn it! This was not happening to her. She'd bathed in Japan in front of strangers and had thought nothing of it. She'd once followed the French fashion of sunbathing topless on a beach in Monaco. She wasn't hung up on nudity. So why was she blushing like a schoolgirl?

Get a grip. When she did, she saw that Nicholas had turned his attention to Dimitri.

The boy didn't seem the least perturbed by Nicholas' frown of disapproval. A glance at the king, and she immediately knew why. He was too busy trying not to laugh at her predicament to discipline the kids.

Nicholas spoke over his shoulder. ''Sophia, I've found them.'' To Ericka he said, ''I've tried to convince her to hire a nanny but she insists on caring for the children herself.''

Sophia, King Zared I's widow, was a thin, dark-haired woman with gorgeous skin, dressed in a simple but elegant blouse and skirt. She ducked past Nicholas and stood behind her sons. ''I am so sorry. The baby was crying, and I turned my back on these two. They have a habit of exploring. I'm afraid privacy and security concerns don't mean much to them yet.''

''It's okay,'' Ericka told her, thinking that even this luxurious bathroom couldn't hold another soul. She was wrong.

Tashya barged in, followed by a tall man with dark hair who looked like a younger version of Nicholas. The second oldest brother, Alexander, blue eyes twinkling, carried a baby over his shoulder. Alexander took in Ericka's wet hair, bare feet, the water draining from the tub and threw back his head and laughed.

Ericka realized there could be drawbacks to having a large family, too. She wasn't accustomed to everyone talking about everyone or prying into one another's business or sharing embarrassing moments.

Tashya elbowed Alexander in the gut. ''This is not funny. Stop snickering at our guest before she decides she wants no part of this family." Alexander paid no attention to his sister's scolding. "You better be careful or she can retaliate in her newspaper, tell all the women you've taken a vow of celibacy perhaps," she teased.

Was it just a half hour ago that Nicholas had sneaked Ericka through the private entrance so she wouldn't have to meet his family in wet clothes? Now she stood before them dripping wet, in only a towel.

As if sensing her discomfort, but clearly trying to keep back a laugh himself, Nicholas gestured with his hand for his brother to go. "You can leave now."

"Okay," Alexander nodded agreeably, but he kept chuckling, and he didn't move an inch, his broad shoulders blocking the doorway.

"Tashya, get our brother out of here," Nicholas ordered with just a little more heat.

Tashya tugged on Alexander's arm. He still didn't budge. She let out an exasperated sigh. "In case you haven't noticed, he's bigger than me, and stronger than me, and more stubborn than me, and no doubt he will—"

"If you don't move him," Nicholas raised an eyebrow but not his voice, "I'll marry you off to the prince of—"

"Okay. Okay. We were just going." Tashya reached up and tweaked Alexander's ear.

"Ow," he complained, and the baby giggled as Tashya dragged them from the crowded bathroom.

Ericka, Nicholas, Sophia and the two boys still remained. Sophia leaned over, took each boy by the hand. "Tell Miss Ericka that you are sorry."

"We didn't do anything bad," Dimitri muttered.

"Yes, you did." Nicholas kneeled down by the little boy and looked him in the eye. "It's bad manners to enter a lady's bathroom without permission."

"I thought she was dead. She wasn't moving."

The child was so sincere that Ericka couldn't hold back a chuckle.

Sophia threw up her hands in exasperation. "Dimitri, what have I told you about wandering around the beach house?"

"I forgot."

"Dimitri!" Sophia shook her head and glanced up at Ericka with a my-kid-is-cute-but-impossible look. "I'm really sorry." She scooped Kita onto her hip, seized Dimitri by the hand and yanked them both out of the bathroom.

With almost everyone gone, Ericka should have felt as though she had more room, not less, but Nicholas seemed to fill the entire space. He'd changed into immaculate riding attire that made his long legs appear longer, his broad chest broader. Although his hair remained damp, he'd run a comb through it, and he seemed to have shaved. She on the other hand wore only a towel. He looked unruffled and completely in control, while she felt as if the room didn't have enough oxygen to breathe.

"Nicholas, why didn't palace security stop those boys?"

"Security mostly guards the perimeter."

"So once someone's inside, they have free access to the rest of the quarters?"

"Here?"

"No, at the palace."

"It's the same there except for the royal office and my quarters which have additional guards stationed nearby. Why?"

"I was just thinking about how easily your brothers entered my room."

Nicholas frowned. "If you're worried about safety, I'll ask Ira to assign you additional security here and at the palace."

"Actually, I was thinking about your father and who might have had free admittance to his quarters."

"We've considered the possibilities." All too sure of his welcome, he stepped closer, enough for her to notice the flare of heat in his eyes, and suddenly she wondered exactly what kinds of possibilities he was currently considering.

Damn, she'd never wanted clothes so badly.

Slightly nervous and needing something to occupy her hands, she picked up a comb and ran it through her hair, tried not to recall him seeing her naked back and bottom. "Your brothers are adorable."

"All of them?" He cocked one lean hip against the door frame and watched her closely.

Well, he wasn't so sure of himself, after all. He wanted to know if she found Alexander attractive. Interesting. Was it jealousy or curiosity? Either way, Ericka figured Nicholas had had enough amusement at her expense and decided it was now his turn to squirm a little.

"How could I not find Alexander handsome when he looks so much like you?"

Chapter Five

"Why are women so difficult?" Nicholas asked his brother, Alexander. Ericka, Tashya and Sophia, and their house guests, Natalie Belosova, the wife of the secretary of state, and her daughter, Larissa, had gotten along well during lunch. His father believed that his advisors worked harder for their country after vacations with the royal family and Nicholas had kept up the tradition. Normally Nicholas didn't mind guests at the beach house, but he would have preferred to have Ericka to himself. And while the lovely Larissa had kept trying to catch Alexander's eye, Ericka had pretty much ignored Nicholas.

Nicholas supposed he should consider himself lucky that Larissa had welcomed Ericka with the polite graciousness her doting mother had probably drilled into her since birth. Larissa had been kind to Nicholas after his father's death and she could have resented Ericka. Luckily, her romantic interest had seemingly turned from him to Alexander.

At least Ericka had ignored Alexander just as much

as she'd ignored Nicholas. The only difference was that his brother didn't care.

Now, as he and Alexander rode, the guards bringing along extra horses for the women, he had a chance to think. He hadn't spent any time thinking about women this last year, not with his concerns over apprehending his father's assassin. He knew his security teams had done their best, but they had so little to go on. The fiasco in the park today had brought back his old frustrations that he would never bring his father's killer to justice along with a heightened sense of danger. Although the possibility had occurred to him, he didn't believe the same person who had murdered his father had been behind the wheel of that car. But the driver could be taking orders from the traitor. So, like Ericka, he remained suspicious, edgy.

In the past, Nicholas had remained patient, but with Ericka clearly enjoying the rest of his family so much, he felt unsettled and sought closure so he could move on with his life. Perhaps his edginess had more to do with his brief glimpse of a nude Ericka in the bathroom mirror than his actual need for closure. She had a fine body. Toned muscles. Curves. Golden flesh. And he wasn't quite sure, but he thought her natural hair color might be blond—not that he cared. She'd look good to him as a redhead, a blonde or a brunette. Maybe that was his problem. Since this morning he had held her on his lap, wrapped her in his arms and seen her naked. Hell, he might be a king, but he was still human.

Alexander reined in his magnificent white stallion to give them a chance to converse out of earshot of

Tashya and Ericka, who were sitting under a bright red-and-white striped umbrella down the beach, and Sophia who was building sand castles with Dimitri, Nikita and the baby. The ever-present palace guards were in evidence, behind the brothers, around the women and kids, and even in a patrol boat offshore.

Nicholas relaxed whenever he visited the Black Sea Coast, the jewel in Vashmira's crown, where European royalty had vacationed for generations. He was eager to show Ericka more of this most excellent part of his country. Tourism had been down after his father's death, but it was almost back to normal.

Here the sea, tempting and hospitable, clean and calm, without any treacherous tides or dangerous animals, was safe for even the youngest holidaymakers. Half as saline as the Mediterranean, the Black Sea hosted century-old fishing villages, energetic seaside towns and plastic resorts, all of them competing to suck in hard currency. Tourists took refreshing dips in the warm waters, shopped at beachside kiosks or availed themselves of Russian vodka, Turkish coffee, German schnitzel or Bulgarian *shopska salata* at one of the dozens of cafés. Others rented paddleboats or hid from the sun under umbrellas while children frolicked in the shallow waters and created fanciful sand castles on the gently sloping beach.

Speaking over the sounds of the lapping waves and the horses' hooves stomping in eagerness to go forward in the wet sand, Alexander still kept his voice low. "Is Larissa Belosova going to cause you any embarrassment?"

"Larissa?" Nicholas frowned and realized his

brother had misunderstood which woman was giving him difficulties.

"She still likes you, Nicholas."

"We're just friends," he denied, uncomfortable.

"She wants more. I am experienced enough to know the woman is flirting with me to make you jealous. Her presence here is unfortunate, the timing bad, but I suppose it would be rude to request that she leave since this vacation was planned months ago."

"I suppose I should make some explanation to Ericka," Nicholas said slowly.

"So if Larissa isn't the problem, it must be our dear sister. Is she giving you a hard time again?"

Nicholas was not about to admit to his brother that the difficult woman he'd been thinking about was neither his sister nor his former friend, but Ericka. "Tashya refuses to consider a political marriage with Moldova's crown prince. She called him a toad—to his face," Nicholas complained, but he couldn't restrain a grin. Like all of Zared's children, his sister had a mind of her own, a stubborn streak as wide and deep as the Danube. He admired her spirit, and yet, her refusal to cooperate with his political and economic objectives lay heavily on his shoulders and made his own marriage that much more necessary.

Nicholas had almost forgiven himself for not finding his father's killer and bringing him to justice, but he would never forgive himself if his country backslid into socialism. To keep his country safe, he'd sought strong alliances through the age-old strategy of marriage just as his father had urged him to do. But not only had Tashya refused to marry the prince, she'd made an enemy of him. Currently the two countries, which shared a border, had no diplomatic relations.

Nicholas had wondered if the Moldovan prince could have been behind his father's assassination, but he had not one lick of proof. It would make sense for Moldova to try to weaken Vashmira by taking out its leaders, and then invade to claim legitimate leadership. However, Nicholas had absolutely no proof of his theory.

"So what's next on your agenda?" Alexander asked, his gaze arrowing between two royal guards to focus on a well-shaped woman in a skintight swimsuit.

"What makes you think I—"

"You *always* have an agenda. You don't know how to relax."

"Not true."

"When was the last time you took a vacation?"

"I was just in New York—"

"Giving a speech at the United Nations is not a vacation."

"I was in Tokyo—"

"To certify our international trade agreement." Alexander's neck swiveled to follow another bathing beauty, and Nicholas marveled that his brother didn't fall off his horse as his body contorted in the saddle. "A vacation is wine, women and song. It does not include work."

Nicholas refused to be sidetracked by his brother's banter. "Father recognized that America is our best bet. Nothing's changed."

Nicholas glanced at Ericka who looked stunning in the riding outfit Tashya had lent her, but then Ericka

would look good in rags. "I should have arranged for
Ericka to visit sooner. We need this alliance with the
United States."

Alexander frowned. "Father made your marriage
contract with her for personal reasons, not—"

"Do not fool yourself. Dad's personal reasons
dovetailed quite well with his political agenda."

"You going to marry her?" Alexander asked him
with a sympathetic glimmer in his eyes.

"Would you marry a stranger?"

"I don't wish to marry at all." Alexander eyed the
breasts of a woman sunbathing topless in front of an
exclusive hotel next to their beach house. "However,
you don't have much time to solidify your engagement
before the coronation."

"I should refuse, and let *you* marry her," Nicholas
threatened his brother, knowing Alexander would find
the threat an empty one.

Unlike Nicholas, who put the needs of his country
first, Alexander had established a more carefree private life that included parties, women and leisure
travel. As usual, the woman on the beach noted his
brother's interest, picked up a bottle of sunscreen and
seductively massaged the oil into her dusky skin.

Since his father's murder, Nicholas hadn't had the
time to indulge in passion or to brood over the lack
of intimacy in his life. He'd been content to remain
single and had had no great desire to marry, although
he thought that someday he would settle down. He
spent his days conferring with his advisors over the
best way to attract tourist dollars, improve health care
and guard their country from enemies both inside and

out. In addition, he oversaw the continuing investigation into his father's assassination.

Ericka Allen's contacts and connections would be an invaluable asset to his country. She had the intimate knowledge of the workings of American politics that an outsider would never have. She was smart, attractive, courageous. And she'd managed to ignore him all through lunch. The thought stung. Women did find him attractive, although they usually preferred his brother.

Alexander and Nicholas both shared their father's height, his broad shoulders and dark hair, yet the ladies gravitated toward Alexander, whose eyes were a lighter shade of blue and perhaps a tad less serious. The brothers might look alike, their chins square, jaw-lines and thick brows similar, but women flocked to Alexander, who loved parties, dancing and music, perhaps traits passed on to him from their French-born mother, Brigette LaFarge.

Nicholas preferred to spend his limited free time on solitary sojourns through the city streets and outlying villages. He enjoyed reading Ludlum and Clancy, playing checkers, and cooking rich French food, apparently the only attribute he'd inherited from their mother.

He liked women. And he certainly liked Ericka Allen. Although he'd always hoped to marry for love—not political necessity, the more time he spent around the American, the less he was opposed to a union with her. In fact, he was looking forward to the challenge of convincing her to stay in Vashmira—however, he should have allowed himself more than a week. What had he been thinking?

Alexander grinned at him. "I'm *not* the best man for the job, and we both know it."

If Nicholas had seen Ericka's picture a year earlier and had known of her strong values and work ethic, perhaps he wouldn't have been so reluctant to meet her, but now that he had, her physical attributes were the least of his concerns. "Perhaps she won't want me."

Alexander speared him with a piercing stare. "Is that what you're hoping? That she'll refuse you?"

Not anymore.

His brother could exhibit a keen perception when he chose to focus his mind, but Nicholas maintained a stoic expression, not about to let Alexander know his jab had struck home or that he'd since changed his mind. When he remained silent, Alexander continued, "Doesn't every little girl dream of her prince sweeping her away and living happily ever after?"

"This isn't a fairy tale," Nicholas replied with more irritation than he'd intended. Where was his famous royal calm when he needed it?

His brother could be very direct. "Marriage and a family will make you appear a more stable leader to our countrymen and our allies. Besides, left to your own devices, I doubt you'd wed before you're too old to sit on a horse."

"I don't see *you* settling down."

"Why should I?" Alexander's eyes sparkled, "when there are so many women ready to satisfy my every desire?" He veered off, heading toward the bare-breasted sun worshipper on the beach. The royal guards assigned to his brother followed. The majority stayed with Nicholas, keeping everyone protected.

Nicholas nudged his horse into a trot, pleased he was heading toward Ericka and not some stranger like the woman lying in the sun. He hadn't wanted to marry an American, but Ericka no longer seemed like a foreigner. She stood chatting with Sophia and the Belosovas as if they were old friends and she hadn't a care in the world. Her curly auburn hair sparkled in the sunlight, her green eyes vibrant.

He rode slowly, thinking through the details. He couldn't move too fast in his courtship—such an old-fashioned word, but the only one appropriate for their situation—or she would discern his intentions and possibly depart before they had a chance to know one another better. Yet, his coronation ceremony was next week and by then he would have to announce his engagement.

Add to his difficulties the ever-present palace security dogging his footsteps and he realized that serious alone time with Ericka would have to be planned as carefully as any military campaign—especially since he dared not dismiss those guards after the problems in the park. Up ahead, guards surrounded his younger brothers. Sophia's dark locks contrasted with the white hair of Natalie Belosova, who visited with Sophia and played with the boys in the sand. Ericka took it all in, Tashya wiping sand from the baby's mouth, Sophia's hands guiding the two boys' efforts to build a sand castle. Larissa had eyes only for Alexander, who was flirting with a woman down the beach.

Dimitri spied Nicholas' Arabian, squealed and ran toward him on chubby legs. "Nicky! Up. Up. Up!"

Nicholas looked at Ericka. "Would you mind some extra company?"

"Of course not."

A guard stepped forward and handed Tashya and Ericka the reins of their mounts. Nicholas enjoyed the sight of Ericka swinging gracefully into the saddle. Beside her, Tashya and Larissa mounted their horses. His sister spun her horse back toward the way he'd come. "I think I'll check on Alexander."

"I'll go with you," Larissa told his sister.

"He may not wish to be interrupted," Nicholas said.

Tashya laughed. "That should make it oh-so-much-more fun." In a moment, she'd urged her horse into a gallop, leaving Larissa to follow.

"Up," Dimitri demanded again. "Want ride."

Nicholas knew that some women would object to his taking the kids along, but Ericka seemed more fascinated by the children than upset. Damn it. He needed her to want to be alone with him, but she seemed quite content with the prospect of company.

He nodded and a guard handed Dimitri into his arms. He'd always been unable to resist the child's boisterous energy. "Hang on, little guy."

"Me, too," Nikita demanded, his arms already up, waiting for a lift.

Nicholas settled Dimitri behind him and Nikita in front of him. Seeing that he'd been deserted by everyone except his mother, the baby, Pavel, began to cry. At one, three and five years old, his little brothers would grow up to be men with no memories of their father. The thought saddened Nicholas, and he held out his arms to take Pavel from Sophia.

Sophia brushed the sand from her skirts. "First, let me put Pavel in the harness."

"I can hold him," Ericka offered.

"I appreciate the offer, but unless he's with his brothers he won't be happy," Nicholas told her and turned to Sophia. "Hand him over."

While Natalie looked on, Sophia handed him the baby, but spoke to Ericka. "At first, I was reluctant to place more than one child at a time in his charge, but the boys insist on staying together."

Nicholas spoke wryly, "So far I've always brought them back in one piece."

"See that you continue to do so," Sophia affectionately admonished.

Natalie waved goodbye. "Have a good ride." Sophia, Natalie and Larissa roamed over the beach toward the house and some shade.

Nicholas attached the harness to his chest, Pavel faced outward and looked around, his bright brown eyes wide with interest at the view from atop the horse. Ericka seemed quite interested in the arrangements. He could almost see her mind writing about the king who played baby-sitter. He supposed he wasn't giving her a very regal picture of his life.

"Got more than you can handle?" she asked him.

"We do this all the time."

"Then why are you frowning?"

"I'm afraid that if you write about them," he gestured to the children, "my enemies might believe the children are a weakness they could exploit."

Ericka rode up next to him, her attention on the baby. "He might be tiny, but he knows exactly what he wants."

Again she hadn't responded to his probe into the contents of her article, but he couldn't dwell on that for long. Not with the responsibility for three children in his charge.

Nicholas was happy to carry them on a ride and to hold the little guy. He liked cuddling the baby—but he would admit his weakness to no one—although he suspected the gentle Sophia had known his secret ever since she'd caught him rocking the baby to sleep and singing him a lullaby. If Alexander or Tashya knew, they'd tease him mercilessly, and he couldn't help wondering what Ericka would think.

Recalling his earlier conversation with Alexander, Nicholas cleared his throat, determined to tell Ericka about his past before the gossip at court reached her ears.

Still he hesitated, unsure how to bring up the uncomfortable subject. "There's something you should know."

She must have heard his tone change because she stopped her mount, her beautiful eyes curious. "Yes?"

The kids were busy discussing the boats and paying no attention to the adult conversation so he felt free to speak. "Larissa and I... Many years ago..."

"Were lovers?"

"She wished it had been so."

"And you didn't wish it?"

"She...how do you Americans say...was too intense for me."

"I see."

Did she? Nicholas could read the unspoken questions in her eyes, but saw no need to explain further. His past was not her concern—not even if she became his wife.

"Can we go fast?" Dimitri asked and Nicholas was grateful for the interruption.

"Horse go swimming," Nikita demanded.

Pavel contentedly sucked his thumb, and Nicholas wished all problems could be solved so easily as keeping his little brothers happy. Again he glanced at Ericka, but had no idea what she was thinking. He knew so little about this woman that he was contemplating spending the rest of his life with and regretted that he hadn't made an effort to get to know her sooner. After the incident in the park he supposed he should count himself lucky that she hadn't marched back onto the plane and left his country and him without a backward look. However, he would just have to make up for the limitations and lost time by being more direct than usual. "Do you want children?"

"Someday."

"What about your career?"

"Haven't you heard? This is the new millennium. Women now have children and careers."

"Yours requires lots of travel." He gave her another glance, admiring the way she sat tall in the saddle. Her expression and easy answers told him she was comfortable with his personal questions, revealing that she'd obviously considered these issues, and had likely made some plans, too.

"When the time comes, I can ask for a permanent assignment to D.C."

"You've given this some thought." Although she'd told him she didn't have a husband, he was beginning to wonder if she had someone specific in mind. "Anyone special at home?"

She suddenly tensed and answered him way too casually for him not to realize she'd raised her defenses. "Not at the moment."

She might be wary, but relief washed over him. He could discount the possibility of having competition from a lover she'd left at home. It was difficult enough that he wanted her to marry him and give up her country and her job, but if another man was in her thoughts, his task would be impossible.

All he needed was for her to fall for him in a week. He supposed stranger things had happened. His father had tumbled instantly in love with his mother the first time they'd met. Nicholas frowned. Perhaps that wasn't a solid example.

"Now, why are you frowning? Were you hoping I was in love with someone?" she asked with keen perception.

"Actually, I was recalling how my father told me that he fell instantly in love with my mother." The boys sat happily and quietly on the horse, the baby content to dangle from the harness strapped to Nicholas' chest. The silent peacefulness wouldn't last, but for now his little brothers were content to simply gaze at the sail- and powerboats cruising, one pulling a water-skier, over the calm blue sea.

Ericka leaned over and straightened Dimitri's hat, so the sun didn't shine in his eyes. "They had a good marriage?"

"My father thought so."

"You didn't?" Ericka elevated a brow.

"My mother abandoned him during the revolution. She snatched us kids and fled in the middle of the night."

"Lots of people fled."

"She died from sniper fire, trying to cross the border."

His voice must have hinted at his feelings because she asked, "You consider her action a betrayal?"

"Her loyalty was misplaced. She should have stayed with my father."

Ericka regarded him curiously as if trying to understand his perspective. "Your mother probably feared for her children's lives."

"By *fleeing* she put us all in danger."

"In retrospect, you're right. But at the time, I'm not so sure I wouldn't have done the same."

Damn. He'd almost thought her perfect. So why did she have to go and agree with the actions of a mother he still considered a traitor? Perhaps she didn't understand, and he sought to fill in the painful details as objectively as possible. "My father begged her to stay. He feared that his people would take her leaving as a sign that his revolution was failing. It's the only time I can recall them arguing. She agreed to do as he asked, but when he rode off into battle, she sneaked away and carried us with her.''

''You've never forgiven her, have you?''

He didn't respond since he didn't want her to write his answer in her article. ''She made my father's job more difficult. When word got out that she'd fled, our enemies strengthened their resolve and the fighting escalated. It's impossible to estimate how many people died due to her cowardice.''

''That's a little harsh.''

''You sound like Tashya. I just wonder…''

''What?''

''If she would have fled if Vashmira had been her native country.'' The moment the words came out of his mouth, he wanted to recall them. He wasn't usually so careless around reporters, but for some reason he found Ericka easy to talk to and he very much wanted her to understand. But he may have insulted the woman. Ericka was also a foreigner.

''Nicholas.''

''Yeah?''

He expected her to be somewhat upset with him, tell him he was wrong.

''Nikita is going to swallow those reins if you don't pull them out of his mouth.''

''Good,'' Nikita said through a mouthful of leather.

Nicholas couldn't have been more thankful for his little brother's distraction. ''He's teething, but he won't hurt the leather.''

''It's not the leather I'm concerned about. How sanitary can horse reins be?''

He patted Nikita's head fondly. "I used to do the same thing."

She shook her head, her tone light. "Oh, well then, since *you* used to do it, it must be fine."

"Are you mocking me, woman?"

Before she could answer, Dimitri pointed at the water between a patrol boat and a pleasure craft. "Can we swim the horse?"

"Not today. In fact, it's time we turned back." Nicholas used his knees to guide his mount since Nikita had the reins in his mouth. "They love riding, but sitting still for more than twenty minutes is difficult for them."

"Okay." The moment she turned her horse, her mare started to prance. She held the animal in but clearly the horse longed to run.

"Go ahead," Nicholas told her. "I'll meet you in a few minutes." He nodded to a security guard to follow her and looked forward to watching her handle the horse. He had no doubts she would make the animal obey her commands.

"Boat," Nikita said.

Nicholas kept his gaze on Ericka. "Yes, there are lots of boats."

Ericka eased up on her reins, all the encouragement her horse required to break into a canter. In total control, she moved with the animal as if she'd been born in the saddle. Wind whipped her hair, and he wished he could see more of her than her straight back and firm derriere, although watching her bottom nestle into the saddle reminded him how good it had felt against his lap.

"Boat," Nikita said, again.

Nicholas had always appreciated the sight of a skilled woman rider on a horse. And Ericka now provoked wonderful images. He imagined her eyes lit with excitement, her cheeks flushed with pleasure.

Dimitri tugged on his sleeve. "Boat."

This time, Nicholas realized that a speedboat was heading in toward the beach. The pleasure craft had crossed the path of the warning buoys that cautioned boaters not to approach the shoreline or trespass. The palace boat's engines roared into life and the armed security detail turned on the siren, chasing the pleasure craft.

The driver ignored the warning.

Nicholas' guards fanned out, positioning themselves between him and the boat. Nicholas didn't like his and his brothers' vulnerable position on the beach. With one child in front of him on the saddle and another behind and the baby strapped to his chest, Nicholas didn't dare break into a trot.

Heading inland wasn't an option—not with the hotels on this end of the beach and innocent people sunbathing.

At the siren's alarm, Alexander had leapt into his saddle, but he remained too far away to reach Nicholas and the children before the boat beached itself—even at a wild gallop. Tashya was even farther away but that didn't stop her from trying to ride closer either. However, Larissa had taken one look at the danger and ridden for the stables.

Surely the driver would heed the palace security boat and turn back soon. His security guards on shore had drawn their weapons, stationing themselves between the oncoming boat and their king. The driver didn't so much as flinch a muscle or turn his head but kept driving at full speed. Fear for the children bit at his spine as he guessed that the driver intended to use the boat as a missile.

His men opened fire on the driver, their shots shattering the glass windshield and chipping the hull. But the boat raced forward at full speed.

Ericka glanced toward the oncoming boat and suddenly she changed direction. Wheeling her horse around, she galloped back to him, her face set with determination, her eyes wide with worry. Within seconds, she'd reached him and had drawn her horse to a halt, spraying sand.

''Give me Nikita,'' she demanded, her voice calm but authoritative.

Nicholas hoped the boat would stop or sink in the hailstorm of bullets. But the boat just kept charging. At full throttle, it would ram way up onto the shore. But where? How far up would the boat beach itself?

After seeing Ericka handle her mount, Nicholas had no qualms about handing a child over to her. Placing Nikita before her in the saddle, she clamped one arm around his little waist. Nicholas swung Dimitri around to his hip where he could support him with one arm, used his other arm to hold the baby's head protectively against his chest, thankful his horse would follow knee commands.

He exhorted his horse into a gentle canter after Ericka, automatically calculating the angles and speed needed to avoid the boat zooming inland. Whichever way he rode, the boat seemed erratically to change angles and follow. It had to be an optical illusion because the driver had gone down.

Nicholas' horse gained on Ericka's mare, the stallion's long stride eating up the distance between them.

The boat accelerated and seemingly changed direction again, cutting them off from palace security, Alexander and Tashya.

Something niggled in the back of Nicholas' mind, the scent of gasoline, the danger of it igniting. Something about the relentlessly pursuing boat with no driver made his perceptions more acute. With the baby strapped to his chest and Dimitri in his arms, he leapt off his horse, deliberately colliding with Ericka and Nikita. All five of them tumbled to the ground. The horses, free of their riders, galloped straight back to the stable and safety.

Somehow he managed to land on his back, cradling Dimitri and the baby. He turned his head toward Ericka and Nikita. "Stay down," he yelled.

Nicholas hugged the babies tight to him.

Landfall barely slowed the boat's fury. The engine thundered, chips of paint flew from the hull, the propellers spitting sand, the boat's speed deadly.

His brothers! Nicholas held them close, knowing he could do no more to protect them and Ericka.

Eyes narrowed against the stinging sand, heart pounding with the futility of their efforts to escape, adrenaline coursing hotly through his blood, he watched the boat veer straight toward them like a heat-seeking missile to its target.

Chapter Six

Although Ericka hadn't expected Nicholas to knock her from her horse, years of riding had her automatically kicking her feet free of the stirrups and tumbling sideways to avoid flailing hooves. She smacked into the beach with enough force to knock the wind from her chest. She'd twisted in the air and avoided squashing Nikita.

She cuddled the boy in the crook of her arm, tugging him closer to her side in an attempt to protect him from danger. The boat had finally ground to a stop about fifty yards away. She was about to shove to her feet when Nicholas' arm pressed her flat.

Before she could ask what the hell he was doing, an explosion rocked the beach, lifting up their bodies, then bouncing them into the ground, showering them with sand and fiberglass pieces from the boat's blackened hull. Her ears rang from the blast, and her lungs burned from the heat, the detonation seeming to suck the oxygen from her lungs.

"Hot," Nikita complained and started to cry.

At least he was alive and well enough to complain.

Ericka sat up slowly, her gaze going first to the little boy. He had a scrape on one cheek, and she ran her hands over his limbs to reassure herself he was still in one piece. He appeared just fine, but she was no doctor and hoped he hadn't suffered internal injuries. However, from the way he squirmed, she figured he couldn't be too badly hurt. "You okay?"

"I want my mother."

"We'll find her soon, sweetie. Let's check your brothers, first, all right?"

There was little left of the boat except a smoking, foul-smelling hulk. Ira Hanuck, the chief of security, issued orders, and palace guards obeyed, hurrying toward them, but Ericka reached Nicholas first. He huddled over the baby, his weight on his elbows and knees. She could barely see Dimitri or the baby since Nicholas had shielded the children from the blast, covering them with his broad chest.

While Nicholas hadn't moved, Dimitri was crawling out from under his uncle and staggering to his feet. The five-year-old's eyes, wide with curiosity and fear, took in the carnage around them with a quivering lower lip.

"What happened?" he demanded, his voice childlike, but his eyes narrowed, revealing the soul of someone wise beyond his years.

"Boat!" Nikita pointed.

Ericka gently rolled Nicholas over. The baby, still strapped to his chest in the carrier, didn't move. His tiny eyes were closed, his cheeks pale, and she reached out to unzip him. In a flash, the baby let out a piercing wail that made her jerk back with surprise that one so small could make so much noise.

Relief zinged through her. She'd never been so happy to hear a baby's cry in her life. She snagged him from the carrier and handed him to the first security guard who arrived. The baby promptly placed his thumb in his mouth but kept crying.

Kneeling, she frowned with worry over Nicholas sprawled in the sand. If he hadn't pulled them down before the blast, it was likely they would all be dead. Even unconscious, he'd protected the little ones, landing curled around his brothers. She realized she owed him her life, too. She only hoped she'd have the opportunity to thank him. His swarthy skin looked pale and blood trickled from under his hairline. If he breathed at all, she couldn't tell.

A dead man couldn't bleed, could he? Damn him! He was too young to die, too vital a man to have his life cut short. During the time she'd spent with Nicholas, she'd come to respect him. He genuinely cared for his people, loved his country, adored his brothers. And he'd touched the feminine part of her that she had rarely acknowledged.

She spoke softly to the palace guard, trying to conceal her worry for the children's sake. "I think the baby's okay, but Nicholas hasn't moved."

As if to prove her wrong, Nicholas' chest heaved, and he groaned. He opened one eye and stared at her. "I was hoping for some mouth-to-mouth resuscitation."

A moment ago she was ready to thank him for saving their lives. Now she had to restrain herself from kicking sand into his arrogant grin for worrying her for no reason. That he could provoke such a violent reaction from her told her she was already in deeper emotionally than she would have liked. Although she didn't want to see anyone die, she had done so many times during the course of her work. Yet never before had she reacted so unprofessionally to a man. That she could hide her response from him didn't make her feel any better—because she could no longer hide her growing feelings for him from herself.

"Mother," Nikita demanded again, this time his voice closer to a wail.

The baby continued to cry, and Nicholas stood and took him from the security guard. The volume of his cries immediately diminished but didn't altogether cease. Down the beach, men collected the frightened horses and finally someone shut off the siren.

Alexander raced up to them and picked up Dimitri in one arm, Nikita in the other. "Everyone okay?"

"What happened?" Dimitri asked again.

Ericka couldn't help ruffling the five-year-old's hair as she checked him over for injuries, but he seemed just fine. "You have the makings of a fine reporter." She took in the burning boat that the palace guards were cordoning off like a crime scene. The sharp scent of cordite and smoke hung in the air and cast a pall over the sunny beach. "What did happen?"

As if on cue, Ira drew Nicholas aside and whispered, "Your Majesty, there was no driver."

Ericka was close enough to overhear their conversation. However, with the security teams coming and going, and the reporters already starting to gather, she doubted the two men realized she was listening with all the chaos around them.

"The boat was driven by remote control?" Nicholas asked.

"I'm afraid so. Maybe we can trace some of the pieces, but I am not hopeful."

No body to trace through blood or fingerprints, Ericka thought, automatically snapping into reporter mode. Only tiny pieces of fiberglass and maybe a few engine parts seared by the explosion were not much to go on. Finding whoever had done this had just become much more difficult.

Skirts flying, Sophia came running up to her children. Ira and Nicholas broke apart and Nicholas rejoined the others. Sophia, tears of terror streaming down her cheeks, hugged her children. Natalie, wisps of her white hair loose from her normally neat bun, hung back with Larissa, mother and daughter embracing. Ericka could hear Alexander reassure Sophia that her kids were fine just as Nicholas placed an arm over her shoulders and drew her aside.

Nicholas led Ericka away from the happy reunion, no doubt so he couldn't be overheard. She wished she had a camera and then chided herself for thinking like the reporter she was. But it would be difficult to convey with words how kingly he looked at that moment.

He had a small trickle of blood running down his temple and sand plastered to the side of his brow and cheek. But his eyes were full of concern for his family and probably his country. The tight line of his mouth revealed much more than his words. "It was an accident."

She shrugged out from under his arm, the previous spurt of adrenaline sparking her fiery anger. "Don't lie to me. I heard your conversation with Ira. That was no accident." She kept her voice down for the children's sake, but allowed her tone to carry her outrage. "I'd say that was an assassination attempt." She arched her brow. "Unless I missed one while I was taking my bath, that was the second attempt on your life since I've arrived. Who wants you dead, Nicholas?"

"I don't know."

"You don't know, or you don't want to tell me?" she asked with enough bite to reveal her vast irritation at his attempt to deceive her.

"If I knew, do you think I'd allow this to continue?" His voice cooled to a frigid whisper she hadn't heard before. "Do you believe I'd jeopardize your life or the lives of my brothers?"

"So why lie to me?"

He faced her and placed one hand on each of her shoulders. "I don't want to read about this in tomorrow's newspaper."

Too bad. Reporting this story was her job, and she'd be crazy even to consider keeping it under wraps. "You ever hear of freedom of the press?"

"In Vashmira, we don't call such liberties freedom, but foolishness."

"Excuse me," she drew herself up very straight and looked into his bleak expression, her anger boiling at his insult. How dare he call her work foolish? "Perhaps you should elaborate before I pack my bags and leave."

''You cannot leave.''

''Watch me.'' Furious, she spun around on her heel, giving him her back.

Before she'd paced two steps, his hand clamped on her shoulder and turned her around. She glared at him.

He scowled. ''Let me rephrase that.'' His face looked as though he'd eaten nails for breakfast, hard and uncompromising as any medieval warrior's. ''I will not permit you to leave my country.''

She sensed that he'd meant every word, and she began to shake from fury. How dare he tell her what to write? How dare he assume she wouldn't investigate an attempt on his life? Damn him. Only by exerting the utmost control did she refrain from slapping him across the face. He had not just threatened her, he'd laid down the law, and she reminded herself that he held the power to hold her in Vashmira indefinitely like some barbarian king.

''You'd hold me a prisoner in your country to suppress a story?''

''If by running that story you risk the lives of my brothers, then yes, I'll hold you here.'' He softened both his expression and his tone. ''But I'm hoping you'll be reasonable.''

''Reasonable?'' Her pulse skyrocketed. No doubt he was unaccustomed to being told *no*. In fact, she doubted he knew the meaning of the word. Well, he would soon discover she was not some Vashmiran subject to yield to his every whim. She took her career very seriously. ''By reasonable, I suppose that means agreeing with every word you say, Your Majesty? Perhaps you'd like to write the story yourself, Your Majesty?''

''Yelling at the king is not what I call being reasonable,'' he teased.

She was way too angry to fall for his attempt at charm. ''*You* are hoping that *I* will be reasonable.'' She sputtered the words as fury rose up to choke her. What manner of man was this to save her life one moment then try to intimidate her the next? Drawing a deep breath, she forced herself to count to ten. However much she wanted to yell at him, she sensed logic would work better. ''How could writing my story possibly increase the danger to your brothers?''

''There are many people in this country who don't agree with the way I rule,'' he started to explain.

''And do you threaten all of them, too?'' She asked the question with a scathing disregard for his power over her and enjoyed seeing him flinch at her accusation.

He kept his tone measured and calm but she heard the inflexible steel beneath. ''Your story could encourage certain factions to plot rebellion.''

His calm annoyed her all the more. ''Maybe you need a rebellion. The next king might allow freedom of the press.''

''Oh, for heaven's sake, woman. Think. The people's need to know is not the highest priority in the land.''

''Not in *your* land,'' she countered hotly.

''Look, remember Columbine High School?''

The sudden change of topic threw her. That he could have been so knowledgeable about two unstable teenagers in Colorado who had shot and killed their classmates and planned to blow up their school had nothing to do with freedom of the press.

She glared at him. ''And what is your point?''

''If the press hadn't reported the incident, glorified the deaths, maybe other teenagers wouldn't have copied the act. Lives could have been saved, but you Americans act as if the right to know is more important than keeping your own children safe in their schools.''

''That's unfair.''

''Is it?'' he demanded.

Alexander, minus the children, had joined them during their argument. Ericka was too angry to care that their words must have carried down the beach. So what if he knew that Nicholas intended to keep her here and prevent her from filing this story? As far as she was concerned, the more people who knew about their disagreement, the better the chances of the cover-up leaking back to the United States.

Alexander placed a hand on his brother's shoulder. ''I couldn't help hearing the argument.''

''We weren't arguing,'' Nicholas told his brother.

''Really,'' Ericka cocked her head to the side, planted her fists on her hips and scowled at Nicholas. ''What would you call it when the king issues commands that I refuse to accept?''

Alexander looked from Ericka to Nicholas, his flashing eyes revealing amusement. ''Sounds like an argument to me.''

''Go away,'' Nicholas told his brother, not once taking his gaze off Ericka.

She saw a banked fire in Nicholas' eyes that should have sent alarms ringing in her head, but she was simply too angry with the man to restrain her temper. "Don't you have laws in this country?"

"Our law says you are to become my wife." He shot the information at her with the speed and force of a bullet. "Since you have such a high regard for the law, are you going to adhere to that one?"

Alexander frowned at his brother. "Way to go, brother. That had to be the most romantic proposal of all time."

"Didn't I tell you to go away?"

So Nicholas hadn't forgotten about the marriage contract. Damn. Damn. Double damn. Ericka glared at Nicholas, the tension so palpable between them a stranger would have backed away. She should have listened to her first instinct to run from this country. But no, she had to have this story, had to cover the coronation, had allowed her curiosity to put her into danger and an impossible situation.

"Why don't you just kiss her and get it over with?" Alexander suggested with a grin.

"Alexander, if you don't leave, I'll arrange for you to serve as ambassador to Siberia," Nicholas told him, his voice stern, but an undertone of amusement in his tone spiked her anger. They were acting as if this was some huge game, not as if lives were at stake.

It didn't take a rocket scientist to figure out who had the most to gain if the bomb had killed Nicholas. That would be the next man in line for the throne—namely Alexander. Nicholas' brother had been on the beach during the attack, far enough away for him to have used a remote control device, yet close enough to watch the action. And he had motive—for if Nicholas died, he would become king.

Yet, Ericka had trouble believing that the good-natured Alexander, who was interested in women and parties, would be plotting to take over the throne. Perhaps his easygoing demeanor was simply a ruse—but if so, he'd missed his calling as an actor.

Alexander shrugged. ''Fine, Nicholas, I'll leave your future in your oh-so-incapable hands. Just remember that the woman you are failing to intimidate just risked her life to save our brothers. You've repaid her by refusing to let her do her job and threatening to marry her.'' He rolled his eyes toward the heavens. ''I just can't imagine why she's upset with you.''

Alexander must have seen Nicholas' expression narrow to a fierce scowl because he lifted his hands into the air. ''Okay, okay. I know when I'm not wanted. I was just leaving.''

''So am I.'' Ericka started to walk away, knowing she needed to give her boiling temper time to cool, knowing she had a lot to think about. She knew from experience that a close call with death heightened all the emotions.

''Please, don't go,'' Nicholas requested stiffly.

She intended to ignore him and keep walking, but Ira Hanuck, looking decidedly uncomfortable, joined them. Her womanly instincts warned her to escape while she could, but her reporter's training told her that additional facts were about to be revealed.

''Your Majesty,'' Ira stood stiff and straight. ''We need to talk, again.''

"Go ahead."

Ira looked warily at her. "This isn't for the press."

"Ms. Allen won't be filing a story on this incident," he told the security chief with the supreme confidence of a man used to having his every order obeyed.

Ericka seethed and kept her mouth shut. She hadn't agreed to kill the story, and if in his arrogance he believed she would, so much the better. She had established ways of smuggling a story out of a country.

"Why didn't your shots stop the boat?" Nicholas asked the most important question.

"Because the remote control device had special protective armor around it. We've already traced the boat's registration. It was stolen last week. I doubt we'll find fingerprints. This was a professional job."

Ericka wondered from what distance the remote had been operated. Was the person at the controls still on the beach gawking at the smoking hull with the other tourists? Or had he disappeared across the water in a pleasure craft?

"What else?" Nicholas asked, while Ericka bit her tongue. She had a hundred questions but she remained determined not to interfere.

Instead she watched how Nicholas handled the investigation. So far, he'd refrained from giving orders or casting blame and had instead concentrated on gathering information. Intelligent and practical, exactly as she would have guessed—until he'd made those threats against her. Okay, not exactly threats, but enough to remind her she was very far from home and this man's word was the law around here. And that law had promised them to one another since they were children. She shoved the thought from her mind. Now was no time to dwell on her feelings when an assassination attempt had just almost wiped out a good portion of the royal family.

Ira rubbed the bridge of his nose with a weariness that revealed his frustration. "A security camera picked up the entire attack. A playback reveals that either the remote controlled device was faulty, or you and your brothers weren't the target."

"Who was?" Ericka asked, forgetting her intention to remain quiet.

Ira hesitated.

"I assure you, she won't leak this story," Nicholas guaranteed with a confidence that had her struggling to keep her control of herself.

She had no intention of following his orders. She'd been sent here to do a job, and she intended to do it to the best of her ability. She wanted to know who had driven the car through the park and who had controlled the boat. However, even if Nicholas did know she intended to investigate and complete her assignment, he couldn't stop her—not if she came up with a good cover story first.

"We believe the target might have been Miss Allen."

"YEAH, RIGHT." ERICKA'S face clearly revealed to Nicholas that she believed his security chief had concocted this plot to keep her from filing a story about a royal assassination attempt. Another woman would have been frightened by the suggestion that someone was trying to kill her, but not Ericka. She had a strong mind and a brave heart. Nicholas would never forget her ignoring her own safety while she raced into mortal danger to help him save the children. She'd remained calm and clearheaded—unlike Larissa, who had sought only to save her own skin. If not for Ericka's heroics, he would have been forced to keep his mount to a walk, and surely the boat's blast would have annihilated all of them.

So why had he not thanked her, maybe even kissed her as Alexander had suggested? Lord knew, he ached to take her into his arms. Instead they'd ended up shouting at one another, and he still didn't know how the conversation had gotten so out of hand. Normally he could handle the most sensitive diplomatic matters without resorting to threats. What was it about her that made him keep forgetting her career? Or the reason he'd brought her to Vashmira in the first place.

Yes, she was attractive, but Vashmira boasted many attractive women. Sure, she was smart, but if she was so intelligent, why didn't she believe his security chief?

While Ira Hanuck could be devious, Nicholas saw no reason for him to have lied. He watched Ericka's reporter's eyes carefully, fully realizing that she had never agreed to suppress her story. He would have preferred that she'd simply seen the wisdom of his request, but he wasn't concerned about her refusal. Without his permission, her phone wouldn't work, her mail wouldn't go through and her confiscated passport wouldn't be returned, which would prevent her from passing through customs.

Nicholas realized that the actions he was willing to

take to keep Ericka in his country were somewhat extreme but, he rationalized, he couldn't afford the bad publicity. He didn't want his people to worry over Vashmira's stability. He didn't want to scare away tourists and foreign investment.

Although the local press and paparazzi were already snapping photos, Nicholas could stop their publication—as a matter of state security. While tourists had witnessed the incident and rumors would fly, without press, the stories would be only that—stories, rumors, which would eventually die down for lack of evidence to back them up.

Nicholas had no doubt that Ira was correct in his assessment that Vashmira's enemies would do anything to undermine his rule or embarrass him before the coronation—and that included killing off his intended bride. Yet he kept his deductions to himself, knowing Ericka wouldn't accept them. But why didn't she believe Ira?

"Why are you so skeptical?" Nicholas asked her.

"I don't know anyone in this country. Who would want me dead besides you?"

"Me?" Her accusation rocked him onto his heels. She thought he'd planned her murder when all he wanted to do was have a civilized courtship that ended in a marriage between them? Was he so off base in his thinking that a bona fide magnetism existed between them? Surely she had to feel the on-the-edge tension, recognize the lingering glances, note the subtle responses that signalled male-female interest? But if she did, then why had she just suggested he was capable of her murder? She was being irrational, possibly overreacting because of the close call on the beach. She owed him an apology, yet he could easily overlook her insult after she'd just saved the lives of his brothers. Insulted, yet almost amused by her accusation, he leashed his temper, unwilling to let her draw him into another undignified shouting match.

She attempted to stare him down, her eyes hot, her tone icy. "Maybe you don't want to obey the laws of your country any more than I do, although I doubt you would put your brothers at risk. But perhaps the remote control didn't work as you'd hoped."

So now she thought him an *incompetent* murderer. "You go too far, woman."

Her shoulders squared as if for battle. "I haven't gone far enough. There are many questions that need answers."

"They aren't your questions to ask," he countered.

She stood up to him with dignity. "Asking questions is my job."

"And my job—to make sure you're safe—takes priority." Dismissing her objections, he turned to Ira. "Is the road back to the palace clear of the protesters?"

"Yes, Your Majesty."

"We leave within the hour."

Ira nodded and departed as swiftly as he'd come, leaving behind him a stiff and uncomfortable silence. Nicholas figured he now owed her an apology, but didn't know where to begin. How one small American woman could look so delicate and be so stubborn, he had no idea. He suspected neither a debate nor logic would win her over because they came to their disagreement from different places, different experiences, with different expectations. Breaching the gap between them had him at a loss.

Yet, he would not resort to Alexander's tactics—no matter how appealing kissing her might be. He would not gather her into his arms and kiss her while such heated words remained between them. Somehow, he had to ease the damage he had done without yielding to her demands to go public with a story that could put his brothers in additional jeopardy.

Her eyes flashed daggers at him, but she spoke with a softness that belied her inner strength. "I can keep the story under wraps until—"

"Under wraps?"

"Delay it."

Surprised that she would offer a compromise, he felt like taking her into his arms and kissing her. Instead, he considered the merits of her suggestion with care. They might both accomplish their goals if cooler heads prevailed. "How long would you—"

"Hold the story?" She gazed at him thoughtfully. "Until the culprit is caught and the danger to you and your family has passed."

Her generous offer caused guilt to stab him. First she'd helped to save the children, and now she was offering to hold back her story. In his experience with reporters, they only did that when they expected something in return. However, so far she had asked for nothing.

He took in her serious eyes, the stubborn slant of her lips, the graceful angle of her neck and wondered what she expected from him, as all the while he tried to deny his own wish to stop talking and simply taste

her lips. Again he told himself he would not kiss her—
no matter how much he wanted to.

"Your offer is generous," he said, hiding his interest in her as well as his suspicions that the other shoe
was about to drop. "This way I'll be free to fill you
in on every aspect of our investigation."

She didn't move a muscle in her face, yet he could
have sworn her eyes flashed with satisfaction. He realized he'd given her exactly what she wanted. Like
any good reporter, she wanted the details of the investigation for her story. His admiration for her tactics
soared, and although he'd been outgunned by a master,
the beauty of her shot was that she'd hit the target
without leaving him bleeding.

"You could have been a politician," he marvelled
aloud. He couldn't keep his gaze off her mouth. A
mouth that looked smooth and sinful and very, very,
seductive.

"I don't think so." She shook her head, her auburn
hair floating up in the breeze, the reddish-gold high-
lights sparkling in the sunlight. "I have too much respect for the truth."

He ached to run his fingers through her hair, comb
it back into place just so he'd have the pleasure of
watching the wind mess it up again. "I shouldn't have
told you that the out-of-control boat was an accident."

"No, you shouldn't have. Apology accepted."

She was letting him off the hook with a grace that
made his heart beat accelerate. "And I want to thank
you for coming back for Nikita. If you hadn't—"

"No thanks are necessary."

"But they are." And he lowered his head to kiss her.

Chapter Seven

Nicholas looked straight into Ericka's eyes, pausing when their lips were just a centimeter apart, giving her time to gauge his intentions, to retreat, to turn away, or to say "no." She didn't stir, her eyes locking with his, her pupils dilating, her lips parting invitingly, her breath slightly ragged.

Her mouth, softer than he expected, was warm and welcoming. He especially liked the fact that she didn't close her eyes, kissing him the same way she lived life—boldly and honestly. She met his kiss with an openness that turned him on, a fearlessness he admired, and a heat he craved.

Her tawny skin carried the scent of sun-kissed sand and sea air, promising a memorable, exotic voyage that he couldn't resist taking. But like a fine journey to be savored, he wanted to experience every nuance, linger over the honeyed flavor of her, and he refused to rush. He took the opportunity to thread his fingers through her auburn hair that was like silk, so soft, so fine.

The texture of her skin reminded him of crème brûlée, rich, sweet. He thought he could never get enough of her. And then he didn't think at all.

He simply reacted, gathering her close, deepening the kiss, enjoying her arms wrapped around his neck. She didn't hold back, giving as much as she took, encouraging him with the tiny sounds of pleasure coming from the back of her throat. Her breasts rose and fell against his chest, her hips pressed against his, revealing to her the depths of his desire.

Damn, the woman could kiss.

Nicholas had no idea how long they stood locked together. He lost track of time. He lost track of his location. He forgot everything except the woman in his arms.

Man-oh-man, the woman could kiss.

"You two should find a room."

Ericka pulled back, her face flushed, her eyes slightly unfocused, and he barely found the strength to let her go. But words finally penetrated his consciousness, and when his spinning head finally cleared, it took him another moment to realize that his sister Tashya had ridden over to scold him with amusement in her eyes.

She gestured to the interested spectators on the beach. "Our esteemed secretary of state's wife, Natalie, thought I should remind you that you have an audience."

He'd forgotten. Something he never did. He'd forgotten the local press, the paparazzi, the tourists and his position. He'd forgotten everything except Ericka.

Even now, his blood surged hotly through his veins, and he ached to gather her back into his arms.

Think. With your brain—the big one between your ears not the...

Damn it to hell! He hadn't been this hot or ready to go up in flames since...since...not ever. But he couldn't stop to analyze how Ericka had fired him up hotter than a bottle rocket while the press took pictures.

He might be able to stop the Vashmiran paparazzi from publishing their photographs, but no matter how much he would like to, Nicholas never interfered with the press to avert personal embarrassment. Even if he was willing to stop the reporters, too many people had seen their actions to stop the rumors.

For months his people had been watching his every move closely, speculating on who would become their queen. Gossip would spread like lightning, shocking friends and enemies alike. Nicholas should have known better than to create a public spectacle, yet as he looked at Ericka's slightly swollen lips and wind-tossed hair and eyes wide with passion and wonder and fear, he couldn't bring himself to regret one moment of their spectacular kiss.

Ericka glanced at the growing press corps inching closer, despite the efforts of the palace guards, and she stiffened. She didn't say a word, but she had that deer-caught-in-the-headlights look about her that said she'd rather be anywhere else.

"It's different on this side of the fence," Nicholas told her gently, knowing she had once been part of that pack that shouted questions. As she'd moved up the ranks in her profession, she'd moved on to scheduled interviews, but she had to be familiar with the press' tactics. Still, she'd most likely never been the subject. And accustomed as he was to being hounded, he still didn't like the intrusions into his personal life. Ericka didn't have to say a word for him to realize that she felt as though her privacy had been invaded.

It was about to get worse. To return to the palace, they would have to face the press directly. He was about to put an arm over Ericka's shoulder in the hope of giving her strength, when Tashya caught his eye and very slightly shook her head.

Tashya reached down to Ericka and offered her hand. "How about a ride back to the stable?" She flashed a friendly smile. "We'll leave Nicholas to deal with the press."

Ericka didn't hesitate. She didn't look to him to make a decision. Without so much as a murmured goodbye, she seized Tashya's hand, vaulted behind her without even waiting for an assist from Nicholas.

Nicholas supposed she blamed him for making a public spectacle of them. He should have kept his wits about him. He should have recalled that even his glancing at a woman started rumors in the city streets and hallowed halls of government. He should have waited for a more private moment. He was willing to take the blame because he knew better, because they all could have lost their lives in that explosion, and he was still rattled. But she *had* encouraged him. Her lips had welcomed his. Her hands had pulled him closer. And she'd responded to him like a dream.

Now that he had the chance to consider the possibilities, he realized that the close call with death might have made her more receptive to him. She'd been hurled to the ground from the blast, then they'd argued over her writing the story, then he'd kissed her. He'd barely given her time to collect herself before creating a new predicament for her to deal with. But she *had* kissed him back. Had she ever.

Then his sister had interrupted and reality had hit like a freight train. Ericka had pulled back from him so fast his head had spun. She hadn't even looked at him—she'd simply abandoned him as if she'd just made the biggest mistake of her life.

Now, he was alone. Tashya and Ericka had left him. Alexander was nowhere to be found. Even Natalie and Larissa had disappeared.

Resigned to making the best of an uncomfortable situation, Nicholas, flanked by security, strode forward to meet the press, not the least bit sorry for that kiss, merely wondering how soon it would be before he might have another.

He would refuse to talk about the boat. If someone had wanted to kill Ericka and failed, he could make matters worse by allowing the papers to print the story, possibly taunting the killer with his failure or daring him to make another try.

However, Nicholas vowed to increase Ericka's personal security. She might not yet be a royal, but she was already a target.

"NICHOLAS IS IMPOSSIBLY stubborn, but then he grew up striding in my father's footsteps, so he learned from the expert. No one was more stubborn than our father," Tashya told Ericka as they meandered from the stable to the summerhouse.

Ericka's heart had yet to settle into anything resembling a regular rhythm. How could it after escaping death and then surviving that kiss? A kiss that had knocked her for a loop, stolen her breath, fried her brain. She had to have been crazy to kiss the king of Vashmira.

God, what had she done?

She'd violated every rule she'd ever set for herself. She didn't get involved with the people she interviewed. She certainly didn't make a public spectacle of herself. And she most definitely didn't kiss heads of state.

What had she done?

Her stomach cramped. She wanted to kick herself, throw herself to the beach and beat the sand with her fists. How could she have been so stupid? If Ira was right, she might have been targeted to die in that explosion because someone feared she might become Nicholas' wife. So what did she do after she survived? Keep a low profile? Go home? That would have been too smart, too sensible.

Instead, she had gone and kissed the king. In front of the press. She might as well have simply painted a bull's-eye on her chest, handed his enemies a gun and offered herself for target practice.

How could she have lost so much control of herself? After her very public display, she would be romantically linked with Nicholas. Everyone would now assume she'd come over here to marry him.

She actually felt sick. What had she done?

There was no going back. No possibility of denying what had happened. She couldn't plead temporary insanity, but that's exactly what it had been. Once moment he'd been standing there looking so fine, his eyes revealing his interest, and the next, she'd been wrapping her arms around him, drawing him closer.

She'd just made the biggest mistake of her life, not so much because she'd made herself a bigger target, but because she'd given Nicholas the response he desired. And she had no idea what to do. She couldn't just apologize or claim it was a mistake. *So sorry I kissed you, Your Royal Highness, I didn't mean it. I was just carried away by a moment of sheer craziness.*

She groaned aloud, wishing she could just run away and hide. How would she face her colleagues after the fiasco she'd made of this assignment? She'd worked so hard to establish a flawless reputation. When pictures of her indiscretion got out, she'd be a laughingstock. No serious head of state would ever again consent to an interview with her. She could kiss her career goodbye.

She sighed at the very thought of facing Nicholas. Just the thought of seeing him made more heat rise to her face. Tears brimmed in her eyes. Tears she refused to release. She might not have kept much of her dignity, but she wouldn't cry—at least not in front of his sister. She groaned again.

Compartmentalize. Put the memory of that kiss away. Here was a perfectly good opportunity to talk with Tashya, and the reporter in her should make the most of it. Ericka had interviewed soldiers on the front lines of battlefields. She'd been in the trenches during a revolution. She'd interviewed men moments before their deaths. She had always, always, always been able to shut down her own emotions and throw herself into her work. Some men had called her ability unnatural and cold, but she'd never been more thankful to turn her mind away from her own problems than right now.

Tashya let out a long breath of air. "I shouldn't give advice, but I'm going to do it anyway because I like you, Alexander likes you and Nicholas likes you," she admitted with breathless candor. "So my advice to you is to go along with Nicholas because he always wins."

"Apparently he let you out of marrying the toad," Ericka muttered, unsure how appropriate it was to be discussing Nicholas with his sister and attempting to change the subject to safer ground.

"Arguing with him does no good." Tashya arched her brows, allowing a glimmer of humor to show in her eyes. "But I know how to sweet-talk him. Nicholas may have a political agenda, but he truly wants me to be happy." Tashya spoke confidentially as if they'd been good friends for years. "And I want the same for him. You'll be good for him, I think."

Ericka thought not but kept her opinion to herself. She didn't intend to stick around long enough to be good for him. She would investigate the bombing, cover the coronation ceremony, and then she was out of here.

Still, the princess' openness surprised Ericka, and she felt compelled to warn her. "You do know I'm in Vashmira to write a story about—"

"That was just a ruse for Nicholas to get you over here," Tashya admitted with a little wave of her hand. "He needs to convince you to announce your engagement before the coronation. As usual, he didn't allow himself enough time, but then he's a man. What else can one expect?''

Although Ericka had suspected Nicholas' duplicity, she hadn't presumed Tashya would so openly admit it. Nor did she see any reason to respond to her rhetorical question. The princess seemed a bit lonely to Ericka, and she imagined that growing up in a household of men couldn't have been easy. While she couldn't help being drawn to Tashya's overtures of friendship, she couldn't discuss Nicholas without making her position clear.

''What I'm trying to say is that anything you tell me could end up in print.''

Tashya shrugged. ''Nicholas has no secrets.''

Ericka disagreed. ''Everyone has secrets.''

''So tell me one of yours.'' Tashya flashed her a challenging grin that reminded Ericka of Nicholas. But she didn't want to think about him right now. She couldn't think about that stunning kiss and hold her own with Tashya, who'd just proven she had a sharp mind and a keen wit.

''I've always wanted to write a political thriller,'' Ericka told her.

''Why is that a secret?'' Tashya asked, her question perceptive.

Relieved they weren't talking about Nicholas, Ericka allowed her shoulders to relax. ''Because it's a huge step for me to take. I'd have to give up the security of a stable paycheck to go for the dream. What about you?'' Ericka asked, wishing she had the courage to ask Tashya how often she came across her brother kissing a woman in public, but she would not go there.

"Couldn't you write the book in your spare time?" Tashya asked.

Before Ericka could respond, Alexander strode out of the beach house and toward them. "As soon as Nicholas can escape the press, we're leaving for the palace."

Ericka almost asked him about packing and then recalled that it would be done for her. No doubt her things would arrive at the palace before she did. The convenience was nice, but it in no way made up for the difficulties—such as avoiding assassination attempts or putting up with the paparazzi or trying to investigate a story in Vashmira. Or kissing the king.

She still couldn't believe the wallop that kiss had packed. She'd resisted placing her hands to her tender lips, but if she looked as disheveled as she felt, Nicholas' brother and sister were being incredibly kind by not mentioning it.

So much had happened during her stay here that she hadn't had enough time to think or to sort out her thoughts. She was eager to visit the palace and observe the royal family where they lived and governed.

A change of scenery, the formality of the palace, should help to put her relationship with Nicholas on a more reserved footing. Just who was she kidding? After that kiss, he probably thought she'd come here to accept her part in the marriage contract. He might even be thinking she wanted to be his queen.

The thought had once amused her. Now it terrified her. She had to talk to Nicholas, tell him she'd made a huge mistake. Kissing him had been wonderful and terrible, and heat rose to her cheeks every time she remembered how close he'd held her, how she'd responded to him with a mindless passion.

Oh, damn, what had she done?

The king of Vashmira was a man of contrasts who both attracted and confused her, and marrying the man was out of the question. Sure, he could be warm and playful, as he had been when he'd pretended to be her taxi driver. He could be arrogant, as he had been when he'd asked her if she intended to obey their law and marry him. And he could be the most exciting of lovers, as he had been when he'd kissed her. But she had no intention of remaining in such a combustible situation.

They needed to talk, and then she would leave. Flee. She needed to tell him that their kiss hadn't meant anything, that she had no intention of remaining in Vashmira and fulfilling the marriage contract. Someone else could investigate. Someone else could cover the story. It had been a mistake to come here. A bigger mistake to kiss him.

She needed to tell him she would forget about writing the story, if he'd just allow her to leave. She shouldn't even stay until the coronation ceremony. So what if the newspaper fired her? Maybe she could get a teaching job somewhere, write her novel.

While she still didn't believe Ira Hanuck's assertion that the boat bomb had been aimed at her, it gave her the perfect excuse to leave. After all, Nicholas believed that her life was in danger. What rational woman wouldn't get the heck out of Vashmira?

ERICKA HAD ASSUMED SHE would ride to the palace with Nicholas, but she'd ended up in a car with Alexander and Tashya. As much as she wanted to set things straight between Nicholas and herself, she couldn't help appreciating the inside look at the royal family and intended to type up her impressions the first chance she got. Meanwhile she filed away mental notes of Tashya's and Alexander's teasing of one another and how easily they brought her into their conversations. Either they hadn't spent much time around the press or they were very naive. However, Ericka had already made up her mind to write their stories by casting them in a good light. She just couldn't believe that Alexander had it in him to murder his father and then his brother, and she planned to keep the ugly suspicion to herself. Brother and sister acted as if they had absolutely nothing to hide. If they wouldn't censor themselves, she would take care to protect them.

The drive took less than an hour, and the palace loomed out of the mist like some storybook castle atop a mountain, hovering in the clouds. With a moat, a drawbridge and turrets, the castle had a whimsical appeal, but served as a daunting fortress. No wonder Nicholas had wanted to return here where the perimeter would be easier to secure. Palace guards in bright scarlet uniforms stood watch at the gates, but she also noted modern security cameras, voiceprint identification systems, and for the guards, headsets with mouthpieces and earphones and bulging jackets which indicated they were fully armed.

However professional palace security looked, they'd failed to prevent Zared I's assassination, which had taken place right inside the royal office. She recalled Nicholas' telling her they suspected an inside job and wondered if the person who had killed his father could now be gunning for Nicholas. In small countries, when the firstborn son was ruling and became a target, the second son had to be the primary suspect since he had the most to gain. She'd thought about this carefully.

After studying Alexander, however, after seeing his concern for his brothers, she just couldn't believe he'd plotted first his father's and now his brother's murder. He didn't seem power hungry or terribly ambitious. In fact, he seemed to be just what the press said he was, a handsome playboy mostly interested in women and partying.

However much she'd like to cross Alexander off her list of suspects, she couldn't unless he had an irrefutable alibi. But there were other people on her list of suspects, possibly even Ira Hanuck, the palace chief of security. Who would have better access, know the chinks in the protection he himself had arranged, than the man in charge of protecting the king? But as far as Ericka knew, Ira had no motive unless he was working with someone else—someone like Alexander?

No, the thought was too horrible. She'd rather not think it. She knew that military coups took place with regularity in third-world countries and they were often carried out by the general in charge of the military. After they reached the palace, Ericka planned to speak with General Vladimir and take her measure of the man.

The inside of the palace which was decorated with a combination of contemporary and antique furnishings delighted Ericka. She knew that castles, while having glamorous images, tended to be drafty places, difficult to heat in winter. But Tashya had informed her on the way over that before his death their father had modernized the place, installing central heating, air-conditioning and new plumbing, as well as luxury appliances.

Ericka's room was in the west wing, a spacious suite of rich emeralds and golds including a domed ceiling painted by Russian masters, mosaic floors warmed with Turkish carpets and a canopy bed big enough to hold a sultan and half his harem. Servants had neatly put away her belongings in closets and drawers. Her laptop waited on a gleaming wooden desk with graceful curving legs that looked as if it belonged in a museum.

She plugged in her computer, recharging the battery, and began to work. Her fingers flew over the keys, typing her impressions of Vashmira, its royal family and especially its king. As usual, she lost track of time while she worked, finally stopping when her neck ached.

She reread the story, editing her words, mostly going with her first impressions. Long ago she'd rewritten every word. She'd since trained herself to write cleanly on the first draft and hence didn't require much of an edit. When she finished she saved and backed up her work onto two floppy disks. One she kept with her computer, the other she placed in her purse—an old habit that had saved her when the Chinese military had confiscated her computer on the way out of

Beijing and again when her computer was stolen in India.

Tashya had informed Ericka dinner would be formal and at nine. Nicholas had invited his inner circle so she would meet the people he relied on to run his country. Although she was still determined to leave, she would make the most of the opportunity. She wanted to meet General Vladimir and those cabinet members closest to Nicholas. And hopefully she'd have a chance for a private moment with Nicholas to ask him to allow her to leave.

She got her opportunity sooner than she expected. Nicholas arrived at her door to escort her to dinner. Wearing a black vest with gold embroidery over a black silk shirt with a black tie and slacks, he looked every inch the king of his country. But it wasn't the clothes that made the man, it was the confident set of his shoulders and the powerful air of command that he radiated when he entered her suite.

His eyes widened with heat as he took in her emerald spaghetti-strapped gown. "Nice dress."

"Thanks. Nicholas, could I have a minute of your time?" she asked, a bit nervous now that it was time to tell him of her intention to leave.

"You can have as many minutes as you like." His words were accompanied by an easy smile, but his eyes gave nothing away.

"I don't think I should stay to cover the coronation ceremony."

He didn't say a word, simply raised his brow, crossed to her fully stocked wet bar and fixed them both a drink. He handed her a glass of chilled white wine, and she wasn't the least surprised to find he'd stocked her favorite—which simply underscored her concern. Staying would be too easy.

She sipped, hoping the wine would give her the courage to get through the next part of the conversation—especially since she hadn't believed one word of Ira Hanuck's story that the boat had been aiming for her.

"Your security chief believes I was the target on the beach today. If he's right, someone doesn't want me here. They could try again—and my presence here could be putting your family at risk."

"You believe that?" he asked with a perceptiveness that made her feel like cornered prey.

"I don't know what to believe, but I do know our kiss this afternoon…"

"Yes?"

"Was a mistake."

"I won't apologize for it."

"I'm not asking you to." Her fingers clenched the wineglass stem so tightly she feared it might break. "But—"

"In fact, I'd like to kiss you again."

Oh, God.

She wanted to kiss him again too, had to use every ounce of willpower not to say so.

What had he done to her? One kiss and she was ready to throw away her career and do it again. She had to be out of her mind.

He advanced and she retreated, until her calves knocked into a sofa. Abruptly she sat, avoiding the opportunity for kissing him again, avoiding his heated gaze, avoiding the need for her shaking knees to hold her up.

"My reputation is shot to hell because of our kiss."

"No one's here, now."

"Damn you. That's not the point. I've worked for years to build my reputation, and in one thoughtless moment, I've destroyed everything I've worked so hard to attain."

"You haven't."

"Once that kiss is splashed across the front page of a newspaper, my credibility is gone."

"So you aren't afraid for your life—just your reputation?"

"My reputation is my life."

"How do you Americans say it? No problem. I've taken care of it."

"You took care of it all right. Did you think I'd agree to stay here and marry you if I lost my job?"

"I didn't explain correctly." He knelt before her, took the glass from her shaking fingers and placed it on a table cozily next to his own. "I asked the press not to show your face or reveal your name."

"You did?" Surprise shot through her at his unexpected kindness. Not that she thought his request would do any good. But he'd done more than she'd expected.

All on his own he had recognized her problem and done his best to set things right. And she'd berated him for it, which made her feel lower than pond scum.

She'd like to believe this was all his fault, but she knew better. He'd given her time to avoid that kiss and she hadn't turned away. On, no, she'd responded like some sex-starved teenager. She could only imagine the look on her face when she'd kissed him, cringed at that image flashing across the world.

"Usually, I don't ask the press for favors, but this is also state business. I asked the reporters to give me privacy until after the coronation. I explained that the pictures would be worth more if you agreed to become my bride but that might not happen if you felt threatened by the paparazzi."

Surely he couldn't be so naive as to believe those pictures wouldn't be sold within the hour. "And you expect them to honor your request?"

"Certainly."

He sounded so sure his "request" would be obeyed that her reporter's instinct kicked in. "What aren't you telling me?"

Chapter Eight

He'd threatened to lock up any reporter who disobeyed his "request" to keep Ericka's face and name out of the paper, but he had no intention of telling her that. He already knew her well enough to realize she wouldn't take kindly to his royal threats. Since he didn't want her to hit him over the head with her freedom-of-the-press argument again, he didn't respond to her question, but he didn't lie to her either, clearly recalling how that strategy had backfired after he'd tried to tell her the boat's explosion was an accident.

He admired a woman with a keen mind. He did. He even admired her gumption when she stood up for her own beliefs. However, he also recognized the inherent problems of allying himself with a woman so conscious of her freedoms. She would fight for freedom of the press even if those so-called freedoms ruined her career. Americans were big on liberty—but they didn't share a border with Russia and Moldova or with Turkey, whose inflation rate would soon destabilize its government. Americans didn't live in the turbulent

Middle East where terrorism often arrived with breakfast and the morning paper.

Too many Vashmiran citizens still longed to return to communism. While Ericka might understand his concerns on an intellectual level, in her gut, she didn't yet accept the delicate balance of social and political maneuvering required just to maintain the precarious freedoms they'd already won.

Ericka shook her head at him. "And Tashya said you don't keep secrets."

"I've taken extra security precautions." He changed the subject to what he wanted to discuss, a useful negotiating technique. "You should be as safe in the palace as anywhere else. So, there's no reason for you to go home."

"There are so many errors in that statement, I don't know where to begin."

Pointedly, he checked his watch, then he offered her his arm. "I shall enjoy rebutting each and every one of your objections on the way to dinner."

She didn't move or say a word. She just speared him with a razor-sharp look that penetrated his composure and his defenses. He had the distinct and uncomfortable feeling that she knew he had no intention of allowing her to leave, but had the good sense not to press the issue.

Rarely did a woman read him so well. Damn. Now that she was so suspicious, he vowed to place another guard in the west wing—not to protect her—he believed that angle was already covered, but to prevent her from attempting to escape, a political embarrassment he couldn't afford so close to the coronation ceremony.

For now, she covered her irritation with an ease and skill that any queen would need to survive in Vashmira. Ericka had a fiery spirit wrapped up in an elegant package. She had courage—had risked her life to help him save the children—but perhaps she had too much courage, she certainly had no problem standing up to him.

Nicholas hated to admit it, but his father had chosen brilliantly. If he didn't love Ericka, he could live with that. She was one fine woman, and he hoped they might eventually love one another, but right now, politics must take precedence. There was only one problem—she wanted to leave. He could see the flash of rebellion in her eyes for just a moment before she'd lowered her gaze. She might be fragile and feminine but beneath that soft and lovely exterior was a warrior-woman's heart that he would have to win over. Because no matter how much he wanted her to become his wife, he wouldn't force her against her will.

Luckily he still had a few cards to deal. Tashya had told him about Ericka's dream of writing a novel. Perhaps he could convince her to stay in Vashmira, become his queen and write the book of her dreams.

Ericka stood and slipped her hand through his elbow. "Who have you invited to dinner?"

"Family and my inner circle. Alexander and Tashya and Sophia, of course. I thought it time for you to meet those people who help me run Vashmira. General Levsky Vladimir is in charge of our military and was one of my father's oldest friends. Peter Surak is my brilliant economic advisor. His wife Janna, however, is overly ambitious and quite disagreeable.''

''Then why keep him?'' she asked, clearly back in reporter mode.

As much as he wanted to speak of more personal matters, he knew she would need this information for her articles. He responded as diplomatically as he could. ''Peter's conservatism keeps me from changing things too quickly and is a constant reminder that not all my people wish to go forward. And every once in a while, he comes up with extraordinary ideas.''

''Who else will be there?''

''My secretary of state, Anton Belosova, his wife Natalie and daughter Larissa, whom you've already met at the beach house.''

''You like him, don't you?''

She could be amazingly perceptive. ''Anton is a good man. And I suppose I owe Natalie, who often fills in as royal hostess when my sister's out of town as Sophia is in mourning. Besides, without Natalie's ambition, Anton might still be a fisherman.''

He had to admire her restraint. Although she obviously still had many more questions about his staff, she didn't voice them. Instead, she held her head high, almost floating down the hallways, and he marvelled at how gracefully she managed the winding staircase in her long gown and high heels.

He'd considered having a private dinner for just the two of them, but after the intensity of their kiss and her panicked reaction to the Vashmiran paparazzi, he felt she needed some room. Besides, he needed to see how she would react to his inner circle. Although

Tashya, Alexander and Sophia adored her for her unselfish act of bravery on the beach, he wanted to test her diplomatic skills. The thought didn't sound very nice, but too often Nicholas had to put the needs of his country before his own needs or even Ericka's for that matter. He couldn't forget that the woman he chose as his queen needed the tactfulness of a skilled diplomat. He wasn't sure the oh-so-honest Ericka Allen had that ability. On the other hand, her kisses might more than make up for the lack.

She conducted herself with immense dignity, entering the room with a warm expression as though she truly enjoyed formal dinners with strangers. But, of course, she didn't know about the sometimes ferocious debates—not yet. Perhaps he should have warned her, but she'd find out for herself soon enough. Besides, he suspected Ericka Allen could hold her own with the best politicians, which was why she was such a respected journalist, and why it would be difficult to convince her to give up that career.

He presented Ericka to his secretary of state, Anton Belosova, and again to his wife, Natalie. Anton smiled warmly at the American, his huge hand taking hers and gently shaking it. Anton's soulful puppy-dog eyes missed nothing, yet his honest expression revealed only friendliness. "My wife tells me you are a heroine."

"I'm just glad I was close enough to offer my help," Ericka replied modestly.

Anton's wife, Natalie, her shiny white hair in a neat bun, dressed impeccably as always in a designer gown, welcomed them with a friendly smile. "Nicholas, Ericka, so good to see you again. I'm glad you are both safe.''

"Thank you," Ericka shook the woman's hand. "We appreciate your concern."

"You've had a rough entry into our country, but I assure you we Vashmirans are a warm-hearted people. If you ever need someone to show you around or would just like to talk, please don't hesitate to come to me." Natalie turned to Nicholas. "Any clues as to who set off the bomb?"

"Ira's working on finding answers."

Natalie leaned closer to Nicholas and Ericka. "My guess would be the protesters had something to do with it. The situation on the streets is nasty and I've forbidden Larissa," she glanced at her daughter fondly, "to go out until this ugly episode is resolved."

Nicholas' gaze found Anton and his daughter, Larissa, who would have looked elegant in rags. She wore some little red number and seemed much more interested in trying to catch Alexander's eye than in saying hello to him and Ericka. Sometimes he wondered if his brother's assessment of her behavior was correct, that her flirting with Alexander was an attempt to make Nicholas jealous. If so, her scheme wasn't working. Nicholas felt nothing for Larissa Belosova.

Larissa had moved away from her parents just before Nicholas and Ericka made their way over. Perhaps she was embarrassed about her cowardice on the beach. While Ericka had risked her life to help save the children, Larissa had only been interested in saving her own neck. Ericka had been most diplomatic about not pointing that out.

"So you're the man responsible for foreign policy," Ericka said smoothly to Anton, accepting a glass of white wine, sipping, then addressing the former fisherman. "Do you think the recent assassination attempt on Nicholas could have anything to do with the Mid-East peace talks?"

"I hope not," Anton answered with an inherent honesty that Nicholas valued. This man read people well and was an excellent judge of character. He clearly didn't mind Ericka's forthright question, and Nicholas relaxed, unaware he had been so tense. His advice was always dead on the money. Anton had great people instincts and, as far as Nicholas knew, he liked Ericka.

Although Anton might have preferred the life of a fisherman, Natalie had done him proud—unlike his economic advisor's wife, Janna, whom Nicholas wholeheartedly disliked.

At that moment his brilliant, oh-so-conservative, economic advisor and his wife, Peter and Janna Surak, joined the other two couples. Peter wore the long robes and turban of his Islamic people and could trace his ancestors all the way back to the time when Istanbul had been Constantinople and the trading capital in this part of the world.

His wife Janna, dressed in a robe that was demure but one size too small, couldn't contain her frown of displeasure. Nicholas refrained from looking down, fearful that he'd see way too much of her jiggling curves. Despite all the official functions she'd been to, the woman had no sense of how to dress appropriately for her age. She dyed her hair an elegant gold but wore flashy jewelry, and Nicholas always thought she looked like a shop girl trying to dress up for a royal gathering.

The thoroughly unpleasant Janna scowled at Ericka. "Dear, a formal dinner is not the time to worry the men with politics."

Ericka's expression remained cool and composed but she raised an eyebrow. "Really?"

"This is the time we socialize. Perhaps you should ask the Belosovas' daughter, Larissa, to show you around, teach you the ropes."

"Actually," Nicholas interrupted, "*I* intend to show her around."

By using the word *we,* Janna had implied that Ericka was an outsider. Ericka didn't so much as flicker one long eyelash at the implied insult. Instead, she shot Peter an I'll-forgive-your-wife-for-being-a-pain-in-the-ass-if-we-can-talk-privately smile. "Discussing politics is a passion of mine."

Ericka had plenty of passion all right. That kiss on the beach had been passionate with a capital *P.* So passionate Nicholas would never, ever forget it.

"I hear you have many…passions." Janna lashed out at Ericka as if realizing that this gorgeous young American woman and Peter had interests in common—interests she didn't share.

Natalie, always the peacemaker, tried to intervene. "There's nothing wrong with passion," she said, giving her husband a loving look as she attempted to diffuse the tension.

While Nicholas could censor the press, he couldn't stop the rumors Janna had so obviously heard about their kiss. He could step in, but decided to allow Ericka to handle the woman.

Ericka sipped her drink. "Why thank you, ma'am. I consider that a compliment." She looked at Peter. "I was hoping for a private interview."

"I have an opening tomorrow. Ten o'clock?"

"Thank you. I'll look forward to it." Ericka ignored Janna's scowl as the couple moved away from them.

"Don't worry, dear," Natalie told her. "She's slow to accept newcomers, but she'll come around."

Nicholas leaned forward and whispered in Ericka's ear. "Well done. I never understood why Peter married that woman." He thought her scheming, thoroughly grasping and unpleasant. The group of chatting people cleared, giving him a bird's eye view across the room. Larissa had found Alexander and appeared to be hanging on his every word.

At Larissa's clingy behavior, Tashya locked gazes with Ericka and then rolled her eyes toward the ceiling. Ericka grinned and Nicholas realized the two women were able to communicate many of their thoughts without words.

"Ericka," Tashya gestured for them to come over. "I'd like you to meet our father's oldest friend, General Levsky Vladimir."

Vladimir, wearing his black dress uniform and polished black boots, eyed Ericka with a stern expression that didn't appear to faze her in the least. The rows of medals across his chest seemed neither to intimidate nor to impress her.

"Good evening, General. I was hoping you could spare some free time for me soon."

"I can always make time for a pretty girl." He spoke English with a heavy Russian accent.

Nicholas wondered how she'd react to being called a pretty girl. He knew enough about American culture to understand that a career woman might consider the general's words an insult.

She grinned. "Great. I'm interested in your increased troop buildup on the northern border."

Nicholas never doubted that Ericka's question was in retaliation for being called a pretty girl, and he had to stifle a smile.

The general's eyes narrowed on Nicholas, who shook his head slightly. He hadn't mentioned any military movements to her.

The general's Russian accent grew thicker. "How did you hear about—?"

"I do my homework," she responded vaguely. "And you, sir," she sliced off the general's inquiry with a feint of her own by turning to Ben Golden, "are Nicholas' press secretary?"

"I'm pleased to meet you." Ben nodded politely, but from his stiff manner, he seemed most wary of her, an odd reaction for the normally friendly press secretary.

Did Ben resent her because she was an American reporter? Or was he simply afraid that she might publish material he hadn't cleared? Many Vashmirans didn't want Vashmira to strengthen ties to the West. But Ben was a moderate. What reason would he have for disliking Ericka?

Servants opened the doors to the dining room and everyone ambled into the room. Nicholas seated Ericka at the head of the table beside him and opposite Alexander. Tashya hemmed her in on her other side. Normally, the family spread out, Tashya and Alexander making sure the conversation flowed smoothly, but as if his siblings sensed trouble, they'd closed ranks around Ericka.

A moment later, Sophia came rushing in, her long skirts swaying, and took the seat at the other end of the table. "Sorry, I am so late. My sons decided to shoot their water pistols in the bedroom."

"They made a mess?" Nicholas asked with a chuckle.

"Not so much with the water guns. But Nikita thought Dimitri should be as wet as he was. Somehow, he attached a hose to the faucet with tape."

"Did the tape hold?" Alexander asked curiously.

"For a while. Long enough for Dimitri to retaliate with the fire extinguisher he pulled off the wall."

Tashya and Ericka both laughed. Nicholas shook his head, remembering the water fights he and Alexander had had and the messes they'd made in the stable.

"You won't think it is so funny if the third story floor collapses into your office, Nicholas." Sophia might be a tad upset with her sons, but Nicholas could tell from her tone that the damage wasn't so bad. Besides, he could have kissed her for helping to relieve some of the growing tension in the room. He couldn't put his finger on the reason, but Ericka's presence had raised the anxiety levels in his inner circle by several degrees.

Or perhaps it wasn't Ericka, but the earlier assassination attempt? Either way, a little levity was much appreciated.

As if he'd just jinxed himself, an aide rushed into the dining room, a note in his hand. At the same time, the general's pager went off. So did the secretary of state's.

Now what?

Nicholas stood, reached for the note and scanned it, aware of Ericka's gaze on him. "Three thousand Russians on our north border have just officially asked for asylum."

Peter Surak jumped to his feet, his robes swaying with his agitation. "We cannot let them in. We cannot afford schools and medical facilities for our own people. Our resources are already strained beyond our limits."

Ben Golden spoke with strength and calm. "My friend, of course you would say that. The majority of people seeking asylum are Jews. Would your response be the same if it were your people asking for help?"

Janna gasped and spoke to her husband loud enough for all to hear. "How dare he talk to you like that?" Accustomed to her outbursts, the men ignored her.

Peter's face reddened at Ben's gentle chastisement. "As Allah is my witness, I don't know."

"Sir," General Vladimir's face looked grim. "One of our aircraft just went down."

"Where?" Nicholas asked.

"Moldova. It collided with one of their planes and made an unauthorized crash landing in their capital city."

"Our men?" Nicholas demanded.

"Alive, but…" The general's gaze moved to Ericka as if he didn't wish to say more.

"But what?" Nicholas pressed.

"We had sensitive intelligence gathering equipment on board."

"It was a spy plane?" Ericka asked.

The general nodded. "We were trying to determine the conditions on our northern border. Three thousand people are living in camps without adequate food and water."

Peter shook his head. "We cannot—"

Nicholas spoke to his secretary of state. "Anton, get the American and Israeli ambassadors on the line. See if they will accept the refugees." He looked at his sister next. "Tashya, what kind of information can you get from Moldova?"

She sighed. "Nicholas, I severed my connection with the crown prince. You know that."

"Reconnect. The lives of our men may depend on your efforts."

"I'll do what I can."

"How many men?" he asked the general.

"The plane had a crew of eight."

"Eight men?" Tashya's face tightened with worry. "I should have married the toad."

Ericka looked from Tashya to Nicholas, concern filling her eyes. "Can't you go through diplomatic channels?"

Nicholas shook his head. "There are no diplomatic channels." He gathered himself, ready to face the crisis, wishing it could have come at another time. He needed to concentrate on courting Ericka, and now he was about to offend her reporter's sensibilities again. But it couldn't be helped. "Ben, brief the press. Ask them not to release the story while we negotiate for the release of the crew. For now, only official palace announcements are to hit the newspapers. I want to keep a tight lid on the story to prevent this crisis from escalating. Ladies and gentlemen, we must avoid an international incident, and I want those men home alive."

"There's more," the general said.

Nicholas didn't let his expression change, but his gut tightened. "What?"

"Our division commander has told me his men will not obey orders to fire on the refugees."

Ben nodded as if he'd expected their soldiers to react in such a manner. But he remained silent.

"No such order has been given to fire on helpless refugees," Nicholas glared at the general. "Has it?"

"No, Your Majesty. But if—"

"If we must protect our borders," Peter interrupted the general, "we must find another way to do it—firing on innocents will guarantee civil war."

"I agree," Ben said with an appreciative glance at his Muslim friend.

Nicholas also agreed. Even if the Russian emigrants illegally crossed the border, soldiers shouldn't be forced to shoot at civilians—any civilians. Yet, Vashmira didn't have endless resources and could ill afford to accept the refugees.

He tossed his napkin onto his dinner plate. "Anton, General, we must find a diplomatic solution to this problem. I want suggestions on my desk within the hour.''

With dinner over before it began, everyone left the room except Nicholas and Ericka. She pushed back from the table. ''I hadn't heard about the refugee problem. Is there anything I can do?''

''Refugees have been trickling into our country for many years now, and we house them, feed them, educate them. Usually we take in an equal number of Muslims, Christians and Jews, so it's not this huge a problem. However, it is expensive, and taking so many Jewish refugees will upset a very delicate balance in our country which is one third Christian, one third Muslim and one third Jewish. As leader of all our people, I must find a nonviolent solution.''

Ericka placed a sympathetic hand on his arm. ''I gather your troops are divided into groups according to their religion?''

''Yes. We have only a few mixed squads. Eventually, we intend to make our army nondenominational—but as much as I would like to force the issue and just have us all blend and think of ourselves as Vashmirans, our groups are too diverse. They eat different foods, celebrate different holidays, and they don't trust one another.''

''I understand.''

She understood? Sometimes Ericka surprised him.

''My country had similar problems during our history,'' she told him with a gentleness and understanding of other political systems that most foreigners didn't have. ''Eventually, we overcame our differences, and you will, too. It takes time and good leaders. You are that leader, Nicholas. I have every confidence you'll find a solution.''

Her faith in him both surprised and pleased him. "What makes you so sure?"

"Because you care."

Ericka's words stayed with him through the long hours of the night, bolstering his spirits despite the seemingly fruitless negotiations. He'd wanted to spend the next few days getting to know Ericka better. He'd felt they had made a good, although somewhat rocky, start.

Now, this morning, with the crisis on the border, he had to concentrate on administrative details too delicate to be left to underlings. Nothing had been resolved, but no shots had been fired. The Russians were at least talking to his diplomats. From Moldova there was still silence, yet according to their best intelligence, the crew of the plane that had crashed on the Vashmiran-Moldovan border were all still alive.

Nicholas could have sent a messenger to Ericka's room to tell her that her meetings with the general and secretary of state had been canceled due to the crisis, but he wanted to see her himself. He wanted to take her into his arms, hold her before he returned to solving another crisis.

He also wanted to share with her the progress that had been made. Although he'd told himself that she wouldn't panic at the first sign of difficulty, she also might not want to live in a country like Vashmira where every day was an adventure. She might prefer a more civilized part of the world. And she might prefer a man who didn't give orders to suppress the news.

Although his edict to suppress the news hadn't seemed to upset her so much this time, he may have again set back their relationship, since once again he'd had to put the needs of his country first. Without newspaper headlines dogging their footsteps, diplomats had more room to compromise. Eventually she'd understand that he had done the right thing.

The closer he came to Ericka's suite, the faster Nicholas moved. He checked his watch and wondered if she was an early riser, if she would mind his waking her. He knocked on her door and when there was no answer, he strode in.

"Ericka?"

Silence.

She must still be asleep. He considered leaving but knew he might not have another chance to see her today.

He strode toward her bedroom, knocked again.

Again, there was no answer.

"Ericka?"

He opened her bedroom door, expecting to see her curled up on the bed. Light shined in the window. Her closet was empty.

She'd left him.

He knew she had gone before he even read the brief note she'd left on the pillow.

Nicholas,
Be back in a few days. I'm off to the northern border to cover the developing story.

Ericka

Damn it! She'd left him. And he'd bet a year's taxes the extra guard he'd posted to watch her didn't even know she was gone.

Fury rose up swift and hard and hot. Not only had she left him, she'd headed for the most dangerous part of Vashmira.

He should have anticipated something like this. He should have known. She'd totally fooled him. And now her life was in danger. A life that was too valuable to risk for a story that would never go into print. He clenched his fingers into fists, aching to hit something, anything, to release the sharp emotions churning inside him.

He'd always feared that Ericka Allen would leave him, dupe him, and now she had. He'd told himself she hadn't had enough time to adjust to their ways, but deep inside, he suspected she would never change. Her independence was too much a part of her nature.

Where the hell was palace security? How had they just allowed her to go?

He would summon Ira and question him, but he already knew the answer he'd receive. The majority of precautions were to keep intruders out, not to keep people in. One extra guard had not been enough to stop such a determined woman. Nicholas, Tashya and Alexander had avoided palace security and sneaked out many times. No doubt, Ericka hadn't found it too difficult to leave, either.

But she was traveling alone toward a hostile border. He shouldn't care so much that she had placed herself in danger. He shouldn't care that she might need his help. But he did, and that he cared angered him all the more.

He hadn't expected her to pull a stunt like this during a national crisis. Apparently her work was more important to her than he had thought. He should have realized no one attained her position without dedication, but he'd expected her to fight with him over her right to do her story.

She hadn't stayed to argue or to discuss or to ask his permission. She simply hadn't cared what he thought. Just when he'd believed they were getting on so well, she'd left him.

Abandoned him. Abandoned Vashmira. She was not the right woman to be his queen.

ON THE RUSSIAN SIDE OF the border, Ericka swore at the phone. She'd already waited over thirty minutes for the international overseas connection and had begun to doubt she'd get through. This might be her only chance to check in with her boss until she arrived back in the States.

"Larry Hogan here."

"Larry, it's Ericka. I sent the story by overnight courier. It's handwritten, but legible."

"You lost another laptop?"

"It's back in…Vashmira."

"Ericka, where the hell are you?"

"I'm not sure exactly. Someplace on the Russian, Moldovan, Vashmiran border."

Even across thousands of miles, she could hear Larry's distressful sigh. "Why do I have the feeling you're in danger?"

"Don't start."

Larry always worried about her, but this time, she might be safer in the hot zone than back at the palace—although she could hardly explain that to him after she'd given Nicholas her word not to speak of the assassination attempts.

"Consider this story a bonus."

"It's not about the coronation, is it?"

"War is close to breaking out, and I'm hoping some publicity might make the politicians think twice."

"What about the coronation and your exclusive interview with Nicholas?"

"It's on track."

"But you haven't sent it?"

"I'm not finished."

"So you're going back?"

The phone connection died. Ericka swore but didn't bother trying to reestablish the link. If she intended to return to Vashmira, she had to recross the border before the shift changed and the guard she'd bribed to let her over the border without a passport or visa went home for the weekend.

Perhaps she should simply fly back to the States. She could make her way to an American embassy. Larry Hogan would wire over her credentials and she could go home.

Although her laptop was back at the palace, she could rewrite the story. She'd never forget the facts she'd gathered about Vashmira or King Nicholas— they were branded forever in her heart.

She should have known when she'd been ready to throw her career away for his kiss that her heart was involved. She should have known when she'd agreed to suppress the assassination story that she was in deeper than ever before. Ever since she'd arrived, she hadn't been acting like a responsible international correspondent but like a woman in love.

Should she go back to him?

It was a measure of how far gone she was over Nicholas that she didn't even consider the coronation story first. Or second. No, first on her mind was seeing if she and Nicholas could have a future together. Or if he even wanted her to come back. She needed to know him better, spend more time alone with him, and there was only one way to do that.

And yet, she already knew how he would feel about her unauthorized trip across the border. He'd likely be furious when her story broke in newspapers around the world.

But she could deal with his anger. She recalled once before how easily his anger had turned to passion. And now she wanted more. She wanted to learn everything about the man, not just his hopes and dreams but how it would feel to have him make love to her.

And she wouldn't ever forgive herself if she ran away like a coward. She raced toward the checkpoint, hiding behind a string of supply trucks, heart pounding. Discovering whether there could be a future for Nicholas and her, a future together, suddenly had her more anxious than ever to recross the border undetected.

She was going back to him—whether he wanted her or not.

Chapter Nine

Three Days Later

Nicholas hadn't heard one word from Ericka. Not a letter. Not a phone call. Yet, she still had to be in his country because he had her passport. Dimitri had seen her leaving—alone. She hadn't been forced or kidnapped, and police had reported she'd been spotted purchasing a train ticket. Then her trail had disappeared. His anger increasing with every hour that passed, he thought perhaps it might be better if he never saw Ericka Allen again.

She'd abandoned him and it hurt. It hurt personally and it hurt his country. Most of all, he couldn't take the pity in his siblings' eyes when they'd tried to comfort him.

Alexander entered the royal office, took one look at Nicholas' furious pacing and shook his head, silently telling him that there was no more news concerning the missing American reporter. "Tensions are higher since we've closed our northern border, but there have been no outbreaks of violence."

"I've sent out feelers to Moldova through our friends in Bulgaria," Nicholas told his brother. "They might be willing to deal."

"Return our men?"

"Yeah but in return, they want—"

"Your Highness," Nicholas' secretary barged into his office holding a slip of paper. "Sorry to interrupt, Your Majesty, but you're going to want to see this." His secretary slid behind Nicholas' desk, accessed his computer and pulled up today's copy of the *Washington Herald,* then exited the room.

"Crisis On The Russian-Vashmiran Border," he read the headline with growing horror. Then his gaze went to the byline, "Ericka Allen," and his rage grew so dark that for a moment his vision tunneled and he couldn't see straight.

How dare she deliberately disobey him? How dare she break their laws? How dare she break his trust?

Alexander's voice warmed with a totally different reaction to Ericka's betrayal. Clearly he admired her audacity. "She not only went to the border and wrote her story, she successfully smuggled it out."

"Damn her! She could start a war with this kind of rhetoric," Nicholas complained as he scrolled quickly through the text.

"What did she say?" Alexander asked.

"She describes the horrible living conditions in the border camps. Goes on to explain how Vashmira can't take them in without causing internal problems and finishes with a claim that the explosive situation must be solved or war might develop."

"I'd say that's an accurate assessment of the political situation," Alexander spoke reasonably.

Nicholas knew that neither the Israeli or American government would be pleased to read this article—even if it was accurate. Anton had been negotiating privately, asking both the Israelis and the Americans to allow the emigrants to quietly resettle in their respective countries. With the debate out in the open for everyone to read, the political posturing would start, lessening the chances of success.

Meanwhile, he would look bad for previously suppressing freedom of the press in Vashmira when his intention had simply been to avoid violence. "Alexander, call Ben Golden. Tell him he now has my go-ahead to brief our press."

"You think that's wise?" Alexander asked, pausing on the way out the door to hear his response.

"She's left me no choice."

There could be no doubting who *she* was. Alexander knew better than to question Nicholas more closely, not with his rage bottled so tight that he could barely keep from shouting. Alexander departed and left him alone with his gloomy thoughts.

With his coronation ceremony in a few days, he'd hoped to bring his people together—not an easy task in Vashmira where so many different people with different beliefs lived and worked. Releasing the story in the middle of a crisis would cause debates to proliferate in the cafés and kiosks. Protesters would soon again find their way into the streets. Enemies on Vashmira's borders would sense the chaos within his country. And where there was chaos, his enemies would find weakness. Violence from within the heart of his country or out on the borders could escalate into a disaster that could tear his country apart.

More importantly, diplomats had more difficulty working together under the limelight of the press. Everyone had to be much more careful to save face. At best, negotiations would slow down. At worst, they'd fall apart.

The Russian army was mobilizing troops across the border. Bulgaria had promised to stay neutral, but Vashmira needed allies. If Ericka's story fomented civil war, if Vashmiran citizens died, he'd, he'd…he didn't know what he'd do, but it would be dire. Drastic.

Nicholas slumped into his chair, dropped his head into his hands. He needed to find some of the inner calm that had abandoned him along with Ericka.

''Nicholas.''

Great. He missed the woman so much, now he was hearing her call his name. If word got out he was hearing voices, he wouldn't have to worry about a revolution, his people would simply have him tossed into the local mental hospital.

''Nicholas.''

''Go away,'' he replied, knowing that there was no way Ericka would be there if he looked up, and he was unwilling to confirm that his grasp on reality was slipping.

''Fine, I'll go. Just give me back my passport, and I'll be happy to oblige you.''

''Ericka?'' Her sarcasm got through to him and he lifted his head.

She stood up straight before his desk, one hand on her hip, her eyes twin pools of quiet concern as if uncertain whether she was welcome, but unwilling to reveal her misgivings.

"Where the hell have you been?"

Her eyes widened at his dark tone, but to give her credit, she didn't retreat. "I left you a note, didn't you—"

"I took you into my confidence, took you into my home, and you betrayed me."

Her eyes narrowed. "My story didn't mention the assassination attempts—only the difficulties on the border. And I *told* you everything was on the record."

He threaded his fingers through his hair. "I expected you to use more discretion."

"Look, I hate to shock you, but my goal in life is not to live up to your expectations. I had a job to do. I did it." Her quiet words were defiant. And honest.

He tried to remind himself that it was not her fault that she didn't fit into the mold for ideal queen of his heart. She came from a culture where women took their careers as seriously as he took ruling his country. It was his bad luck to have fallen for her.

He told himself to take care and then—he spit words at her like bullets. "And it doesn't matter how many people may die—as long as you do your job?"

"Who's died?" she demanded, placing both palms on his desk and leaning forward, her gaze direct, her eyes flaring an angry dark green.

"Vashmira is close to having riots in the streets."

She didn't flinch, as her lips tightened into a grim line.

"Yesterday," she countered with anger and defiance, "I watched a Russian mother bury her infant. You know why that baby died? She needed a bottle of milk." She ended up with her voice breaking in sorrow.

He recalled the visual images from her story, the suffering she'd seen and told so poignantly and softened his own tone. "You can't expect Vashmira to feed the world. We don't have the resources—"

"Other countries do." She slapped the desk with her palm. "My story will cause people to become uncomfortable, maybe struggle with their consciences. If we're lucky, some of them will act. Some might even offer refuge to those poor people—which will solve *your* problem."

He never doubted that her intentions were good, however, she was naive to think that all she had to do was write a story and some white knight would ride to the aid of those people. Until her story had come out, Russia had been willing to let those people go. Now, she'd backed diplomats in five countries into a corner—the result might be that the Russians simply gunned down anyone who tried to leave.

As angry as he was, he couldn't throw that awful possibility in her face.

"We were working to solve the problem through diplomatic channels. Since your story broke, Russia has mobilized their troops along our border. Moldova has refused to help, and our crew have not been allowed to come home. Our Israeli contact has backed off for discussion with his government and the U.S. ambassador is…no longer taking our phone calls."

"Which all might have happened even if my story hadn't come out."

"True, but my people wouldn't be demonstrating in the streets." He flicked on the television, letting the grim pictures make his point.

The news station showed angry people carrying signs and shouting. Some protesters wanted to give the refugees asylum. Others demanded the border stay closed.

"Protesting is a healthy form of political expression," she argued.

"Sure, until someone throws a rock or shoots a gun."

"Look, if that's the way you feel, hand me back my passport, and I'll be out of your country within the hour."

"If you'd had your passport with you, would you have left Vashmira?" he questioned her, almost casually, but she paused to lock gazes with him.

"I'm here, aren't I?" Still defiant, she glared at him. "I crossed the border into Russia and made it back—without a passport. If necessary, I could have made my way into Bulgaria and the American embassy there—without a passport. But filling out the paperwork required to explain losing an American passport is a nightmare. And any explanation could cause you political embarrassment."

"So you returned to the palace so I could avoid political embarrassment?" This was the explanation of a woman who'd just written an article about the problems on Vashmira's northern border for the entire world to read?

"I returned…to cover the coronation. My boss insisted. But if you want me to go—"

"Not so fast." If he hadn't been almost shaking with anger, he might have smiled. Of course, she intended to cover the coronation—that was her job.

He leaned back in his chair, laced his fingers behind his head and eyed her warily. "You knew I didn't want you to write that story."

"So?"

"So, obviously you didn't care about my wishes."

"Wrong." She stared at him and then dropped her eyes along with her voice. "I cared. I knew you would be…upset."

"But my wishes didn't matter?"

"Your wishes as a head of state didn't matter. But your wishes as…someone I've come to care about, matter a great deal."

"Not enough to stop and talk to me before you went."

"If I had made my intentions known, you would have found a way to stop me."

"That's so damn true."

"I don't suppose we could just agree to disagree?" Her words were wistful, soft and melancholy.

Nicholas believed his country needed to come together to solve its problems, and despite the fact that Ericka seemed insistent upon pointing out Vashmiran differences in her story, only history would tell how much good or harm she'd done. What disturbed him more than her politics was her complete unwillingness to follow his wishes.

Every contemplation of the facts told him to end all

thought of a union with this woman. Perhaps if he had not been a king, perhaps if she wasn't an American journalist and they had met under different circumstances, they could have happily wed. However, the way they looked at the world was bound to cause conflicts between them.

And yet, he knew himself well enough to recognize that he would never have been so angry with her if he didn't have feelings for her. In just a few days, she'd touched his heart in a way no other woman had done. She was constantly invading his thoughts during meetings, and slipping into his dreams. Erotic dreams where he held her naked in his arms.

He couldn't allow passion to make his decision. Perhaps he should send her away. Was he simply looking for a reason to nullify the marriage contract?

What would his father have done? Nicholas' own mother had been just as stubborn as Ericka Allen. And Brigette had died disobeying his father's wishes. Not only had she brought about her own death, the children had come close to death, too. Yet, for the first time Nicholas truly understood why his father had never said a harsh word against the woman who had left him. His heart had been broken.

Nicholas looked at Ericka, bold, sassy and sensually appealing, and he let out a soft groan. "What am I going to do with you?"

"What do you wish to do with me?"

He wanted to take off her clothes and make hot, passionate love to her. He wanted to kiss every inch of her. He wanted to take her, right now, right on top of the royal desk.

"I can't see you putting me in front of a firing squad," she said conversationally as if sensing that his angry mood had softened. However, she might not be teasing him so boldly if she knew the direction his emotions had taken.

He wanted to kiss her until neither of them had room in their minds for anything but passion.

"And I can't picture you hanging a woman, either."

The only thing he wanted to hang was a nude painting of her over his bed.

"Oh, I forgot. Vashmira is civilized. You don't have the death penalty here. Are you going to lock me up, Nicholas?"

"How about in my bedroom for a week?"

Her eyes lit up. She unbuttoned the top button of her blouse, her fingers moving with a feminine grace that made his mouth water in anticipation. "That's the best offer I've had all day."

Sarcasm or honesty?

He couldn't read her, but she was playing with fire, and he suspected she knew it. Could she read the hunger in his expression? Did she have any idea of the effect of the images she was placing in his mind?

When he said nothing but reached across the desk, grabbed her blouse in one fist and tugged, her nostrils flared and her pupils dilated. She ended up in his lap, but didn't protest. Instead, she snuggled closer and reached up to run her palm tenderly down his cheek. "Poor Nicholas. It's not easy being king, is it?"

"YOU KNOW WHAT'S THE BEST part about being king?" Nicholas asked her with a huskiness that captivated her and kindled a feminine heat down deep in her core.

She didn't understand how one moment they had been shouting at one another and the next she'd fallen, practically melted, into his arms, but she'd never felt so languid, yet so restless. She also couldn't understand how easily she'd dropped her I'm-so-businesslike-I'm-a-reporter shield and replaced it with a genuine seductiveness that came straight from the heart. While she had no idea exactly what about this man had made her inhibitions and doubts disappear, she was still rational enough to realize what they had together was special—special enough to break every rule she'd ever adhered to—special enough to risk everything, her reputation, her career and her heart and leave herself ever so vulnerable.

The decision made, she could barely think with her pulse skipping and her heart merrily sprinting. Never before had her blood zinged with such urgency that she had absolutely no inclination to fight the desire running through her.

She leaned back in one languorous move and let her head rest on his arm. "What?"

"As king...I can take whatever I want. Whoever I want."

Oh, hell.

She felt so absolutely beautiful when he looked at her with that devastatingly wicked gleam in his eyes. As she gazed back at him, all thoughts of her career, of politics, of her reason for coming here washed away.

He lifted her chin and spoke slowly and clearly so

there could be no mistaking his words. "And...I want...you."

Oh, God.

He couldn't have possibly just said that.... He couldn't know that she found him incredibly sexy, that for the last few days he'd haunted her every waking hour, that he'd interrupted her work, that he'd disturbed her dreams. Erotic dreams, where she'd awakened and found her breasts aching, her thighs damp and her mind full of him.

In truth, she hadn't needed much convincing from her boss to return—not to cover the coronation, but for him. For her. For them. To discover what was between them.

She leaned forward and lightly nipped his shoulder, breathed in his masculine scent, revelled in the powerful arms around her.

"Kiss me," she demanded.

She nipped her way up his neck to his jaw. Apparently, he'd been too busy to shave. The stubble from a five o'clock shadow tickled her lips. And while she couldn't believe she was acting so boldly, she couldn't make herself stop. Not when she wanted him so much she couldn't think past the next few hours.

There was nothing sexier to Ericka than a man who could have had anyone—but who wanted her. A man who had transferred all his anger into sexual heat.

His skin beneath her lips was hot. That he disapproved of her career and her politics could be handled—eventually. Right now, she refused to resist this simmering passion that practically electrified the air around them. Perhaps it was their argument or maybe the power he held over her that turned her on. She only knew that if he didn't kiss her soon, she fully intended to drag his head down to her.

He didn't kiss her. Instead, he placed his hands on her waist and lifted her until she sat on the desk facing him. With his fingertips, he traced tiny circles on the inside of her knee. "There's only one thing you get to decide."

She should have known he would demand to be in control. "What's that?"

"Do you prefer my desk or—"

He bent and nibbled along the inside of her knee. Heat shot through her like wildfire.

Oh…my.

"Or would you prefer to wait until I carried you to the bedroom?"

She trembled. "No waiting." The words had just seemed to pop out of her mouth of their own accord. But then she hadn't really been in full control of herself since he'd pulled her over his desk.

"Such impatience. I like it." He reached under her skirt. "Lift."

She placed her palms on the desk and raised herself, and he removed her panties and hose in one swift movement. She started to unbutton her blouse, but he seized her hands and placed them palm-side down on his desk.

"I want the pleasure of undressing you," he murmured, his fingers tracing a path of fire up her thighs, but stopping just short of where she wanted him to go.

She'd never felt so wanton and kept her eyes on his as he reached to unbutton her blouse. Heat flared, and his eyes darkened with desire. He fiddled for an extraordinarily long time with the buttons, his knuckles brushing her bra and the swell of her breasts, igniting more heat.

She could barely think. And yet, she knew there was something important she needed to remember. He finally removed her blouse and the cool air did nothing to prevent a rush of warmth from rising up her neck. Although it was evening and blinds covered the windows, the lights were on full.

"Perhaps we should lock the door?" she suggested, her voice trembling.

"In a minute."

He unhooked her bra. Sucked in his breath in appreciation, cupped her breasts and licked a nipple.

"Nicholas, please…"

"Umm?"

She spoke through teeth gritted in pleasure. "If you won't lock the door, I will."

He took her nipple between his teeth, held her prisoner. She groaned in defeat. She couldn't move as he held her captive, and then his hands slipped between her thighs, found her warm and wet and welcoming.

"If anyone walks in…"

"They won't." He raised his head, speaking as he moved on to her other nipple. Then he dipped his head, teeth nibbling, teeny delicious bites, all the while his clever fingers were between her thighs, seeking, stroking, seducing.

She yearned to move her hips, to have him, feel him. "Nicholas, I can't…just…sit still."

"Fine." He unfastened the zipper of her skirt. "Lift up again."

She found herself sitting before him naked under the bright office lights. Stoked and primed, she felt lush, voluptuous and very, very feminine. She wanted his hand to dip into her again. She only wished he'd lock the damn door, so she could relax.

"I'll let you lock the door under one condition," he murmured as he left her thighs, parted and aching for more of his touch, and cupped her breasts, using the pads of his thumbs to stroke her nipples.

Her breath shuddered out in a gasp. "What?"

"You promise to come back."

About to shatter, she ached to yank his lips to hers and kiss him until both of them edged lower into madness. Struggling past layers of pleasure, she instead scooted away from his hands before she forgot all about the door. "Like I'm going to stalk out of here without my clothes?"

"Slower," he demanded.

"Huh?"

"Walk slower. I want to enjoy this."

She'd never been shy, but she'd never been this bold, either. Where she found the courage, she'd never know. However, she did as he asked and sauntered, letting her hips sway, even as her knees quivered, as his gaze roved over every inch of her back and bottom. It took forever and an eternity to cover the steps to his door, her heart roaring, her pulse skipping every other beat, and when she got there, she found the door already locked.

She whirled around and glowered. "How?"

His eyes filled with a dangerous heat and appealing laughter. ''There's a switch under my desk.''

''You cad.'' Frustrated, she wanted to smack him for letting her leave when she'd so enjoyed sitting on that desk, as he'd stroked and nibbled her. ''Why didn't you tell me?''

''And miss watching you walk naked across my office?''

Her mouth went cottony dry. The bones in her legs seemed to melt, but she held his fierce gaze, squared her shoulders and flicked her hair back over her shoulder. He wanted to watch her walk? Fine. She cocked her hip and placed one hand on it. She was going to give him a strut to remember.

Oh, yeah. She intended to make his famous royal control snap.

She could do this. She reached up and fluffed her fingers through her hair, arching her back, her breasts rising. She licked her bottom lip, advanced with a model's flounce, placing one foot in front of the other.

''You know, Nicholas,'' she spoke in a whisper designed to whip him into a frenzy of need. ''If you want me to come closer, I do believe you should remove your shirt.''

His voice rasped over her. ''You promised to return to my desk if I let you go.''

''Oh, I have every intention of fulfilling my end of the bargain—after you strip off those clothes.''

''Lady, you drive a hard bargain.''

She shook a finger at him. ''Fair is fair. Take 'em off.''

He had powerful shoulders and a magnificent chest,

wide and deep with the cutest little curls of hair that tapered to a flat waist that disappeared into the waistband of his pants. He unzipped and kicked off his pants without the slightest hesitation. His boxers followed, revealing a readiness that appealed to her on every level.

"Be with you in a moment." He walked around his desk and entered the bathroom. She heard him rummaging through drawers and shelves. He returned triumphant, a foil packet in hand. He removed a condom and unrolled it over himself while she watched, wishing he'd let her do that.

Then he leaned forward and patted the spot where he would have her on his desk at his mercy. She advanced, close enough to appreciate his musky scent, tried to embrace him, but again he placed his hands on her waist, lifted her and plopped her squarely in front of him.

Then he stood with his hips between her dangling legs and spread thighs, his sex teasing her, his mouth hot, demanding and taking whatever he wanted. Tension stretched tautly between them. She tightened with need, arched, trying to gather him into her.

But he would control the pace. Seemed determined to make her wait.

He kissed her thoroughly, slowly. At the same time, he slipped his fingers between her thighs, and she groaned, wanting more. Needing more. Needing all he could give her.

He suddenly filled her, devouring her, his hips plunging and she rose part way off the desk to meet him, matching him stroke for stroke. She clutched his back, grateful when his mouth swallowed her hot moans of pleasure. And then she was soaring, floating, over the edge, her breath ragged, her heart pounding in sweet fury and mind-blowing abandon.

Wave after wave of pleasure stole her breath. Moments later, she felt his release as he tightly breathed her name into her ear and held her close. Slowly, her pulse returned to normal and her brain kicked back into gear, allowing a few clear thoughts.

Nicholas had kept his word, had somehow kept her name and pictures out of the papers, saving her from the consequences of her foolish mistake of kissing him in public, but now she'd gone and made their already complex relationship oh-so-much worse. Only this time, she didn't regret what she had done.

She'd come to him of her own accord, wanting him with every womanly cell in her body. She'd needed to know if the passion between them would reveal deeper emotions. Needed to know if the lovemaking would live up to the promise. To every question, the answer was an unequivocal *yes*.

Chapter Ten

Nicholas stared from the parcel on his desk to the entrance that led straight to his personal suite where Ericka Allen still slept. In his bed. A tender smile escaped him as he reflected on their incredible night together. A night of uninhibited, sheer unadulterated passion.

Damn, they were perfect together. Explosive.

For the first time since Ericka had arrived in Vashmira, Nicholas had a handle on his life and felt in control. Clearly their intense sexual attraction to one another was mutual, or she wouldn't have responded to him with such ardor. And from both his background reports on her and his personal observations, he knew she didn't lightly make love to a man. As far as he knew, she'd never before mixed her personal life with her business one. That she had given herself to him indicated that she reciprocated his growing feelings for her. He was now confident that, given enough time, he could build a solid and interesting marriage between them.

He scrutinized the package addressed to Ericka and

wondered if he would be making a miscalculation to give it to her. Longing to converse with Alexander, but unwilling to speak even to his brother about matters so intimate, he opened his desk drawer, dropped the package inside, slammed the drawer.

He raised his head to find Ericka watching him from the doorway, wearing his robe, which dwarfed her, the sleeves so long they covered her hands. Clearly just out of the shower, with her hair wet and slicked back, her cheeks pink, she appeared younger and sweeter and more vulnerable than she had last night when she'd been a tigress in his arms. He had an instant urge to kiss her, sweep her into his arms and carry her back to bed.

However, they had to work out their differences. A royal marriage could not last if they were compatible only in the bedroom. Marriage required communication on more than a physical level.

She ambled closer and handed him a mug of pungent Turkish coffee. "What's wrong?"

He sipped and appreciated the kick of caffeine. "You look rested."

She shrugged, the robe slipping off one delicate shoulder. "Perhaps we should go back to bed—"

"Instead of talking?"

"We always seem to end up arguing with one another." She leaned a hip on his desk, ignored the robe that inched downward another notch.

"Is that so bad?"

"I'm afraid it is."

She looked so good to him that he wanted to have her for breakfast. He would have settled for a discussion with his arms around her, but he'd tried that last night. Twice. Making love again and again had been the result.

No, he needed to keep a strict distance from her, keep free of her intoxicating scent, her delicious kisses, her eager response to him that had kept him, for once, from thinking about his responsibilities. He still had much unresolved business. He had yet to catch his father's murderer or find out who had set off the bomb on the beach. And his country could be on the verge of war.

"The crisis has worsened?" she asked, with a political perception that made their discussion fascinating and frustrating because they never seemed to agree.

"If we want our plane and crew back, Moldova is demanding an apology and an admission that we violated their airspace."

"Will you——"

He shook his head and did nothing to hide the frustration he felt. "Our plane was on a routine mission over our northern border when the accident occurred. The plane crashed in Moldova by chance. The general says we cannot admit what isn't true. Anton agrees. Peter has told me our stock market is down five percent already this morning."

"And you blame my story for the new difficulties?"

She already knew his thoughts on the matter, so he said no more. Ericka might be stubborn, but she was intelligent, too. Perhaps if he didn't throw in her face how much worse she'd made Vashmira's situation by reporting the story, she wouldn't automatically raise her very able self-defense mechanisms. Eventually she might come around to his way of thinking.

She sat calmly drinking her coffee, her thoughts hidden from him. ''Nothing good has come of my efforts?''

He shrugged. ''We've had some encouraging news. Anton has arranged for a diplomatic envoy to visit with the pilot and crew.''

''They are uninjured? Being housed and fed?''

''For now.''

''Perhaps I should write another article and place more emphasis on the severity of the problem. More pressure on the United Nations might—''

''No. I forbid it!''

She stiffened and her eyes pierced him with a fierce flash of defiance.

Damn. His inflammatory words had been uttered before he'd considered a more diplomatic way to state his wishes. Here he'd been hoping she would come around to his way of reasoning, and she wanted to write another story that could further alienate the parties involved.

Obviously, he knew nothing about women. Nothing about the way their minds worked. Why couldn't she be logical? Why couldn't she agree with him?

She meticulously and deliberately set down her coffee mug on his desk, pulled up the slipping robe, belted it tightly and paced. ''Nicholas, whether or not I write a story is not your decision.''

''That's the problem.'' He tempered his steely resolve with a mental reminder that she didn't respond well to threats.

Despite his having deliberately tamped down his wrath, she kept increasing the distance between them—emotionally, physically. If she'd been anyone else, he would have ordered a guard to block the exit.

Before she left the room, he spoke. "The least you can do is stay and face me. Let's talk this out."

"Why? So you can point out the error of my ways? Forbid me to do my job? I don't see the point." She kept walking, giving him her stiff back.

"Where the hell do you think you're going?" he asked.

"I have things to do. People to see."

He was furious. "You're investigating another story?"

She spun to face him, her face battle tight, her mouth grim, arms locked across her chest. "Nicholas, I'm a reporter. Writing stories is what I do."

"Not anymore." He snapped open his drawer and extracted the package. He thrust it toward her, but she made no move to come closer as if dreading he'd touch her.

Maybe he should touch her. But he knew what would happen if he did. Sparks would kindle and ignite, and then they'd end up back in bed without resolving anything.

"What is it?"

"Your mail."

She glared at him. "Why was *my* mail in your desk?"

He shrugged. "I was waiting for the right moment to give it to you."

"Why is now the right moment?"

He swore under his breath in Arabic, an exquisite

language full of very apt phrases to portray his current rage. "Just open the damned contract."

She elevated one annoyed brow, her tone barbed, but controlled. "How do you already know what is inside, Nicholas?" Before he could answer, her pitch deepened as if she had every right to castigate him. "You confiscate my mail and then you open it? Don't you have any laws in this country?"

"Oh, for heaven's sake. Get off your high horse."

She pivoted like a whirling dervish, her robe floating upward and giving him a look at her trim ankles as she made a beeline for the door.

"Ericka, don't walk away from me." He snapped out an order. She pretended not to hear him and kept going. "Please? I didn't open your mail. I didn't have to…since I already know what's inside. It's a gift."

"From you to me?" She pivoted, a torrent of quiet tears streaming down on her cheeks.

Damn. He'd made her cry. He'd wanted to give her a gift, and he'd made her cry. Guilt speared his conscience and punctured his heart, but from her ramrod straight spine and the glint of fire in her expression, he knew she would tolerate neither an apology nor solace from him.

"It's a publishing contract," he offered since she'd made no move toward the parcel.

"And you're so knowledgeable about the contents," she said sarcastically, "without having even opened my mail because?"

He tilted back in his chair and turned his palms up as if to show her he'd meant no harm. "I orchestrated the offer."

"When did I hire you as my agent?" She narrowed her eyes, clearly furious with him, probably all the more furious because he'd handed her something she wanted—she just didn't want to accept it from him.

"Don't worry, I won't charge you a commission."

She inched forward, glared at him, then the package, then at him.

He thrust it to her side of his desk. "Go on. Read it. You can thank me later."

She snatched the package off his desk and tucked it against her chest as if the papers were as precious as a newborn babe. "You had no right to interfere in my career."

"Look," he ran a hand through his hair with impatience. "You and I, we are too often at cross purposes."

"So you thought that by ending my career—"

"By offering you a shot at your dream—"

"—you could mold me into shape."

"You already have a great shape." He recalled the firm and sensuous contours of her breasts, the perfect curves of her hips, her lovely, long legs wrapped around his waist and refused to acknowledge desire rippling straight to his toes. She was standing there in just a bathrobe, arguing like a queen, and he had to use every ounce of resolve not to show her how very much he appreciated her shape. Instead he offered the lamest of comments. "I'm surprised you never became a television journalist."

"I like to write my own stories, thank-you-very-much."

Sure she did. She wanted to be in charge of every

word, not read a teleprompter. But he kept that observation to himself. "Well, here's your opportunity to write an entire novel, with a seven-figure advance to boot."

"Seven figures?" Ericka gasped and her fingers tightened possessively on the package. "And just what did you offer the publisher in return?"

"You."

"What?" She clenched the fingers of her right hand as if she intended to deck him.

"And me."

"You and me?" If he'd been any closer, her fury would have scorched him. As it was, he still endured a third-degree burn, but he intended to take as much heat as necessary from her if she'd agree to switch careers.

"They want a book about you and me. Us."

"There is no us."

He cocked his head and let her see his skepticism. "Do you really believe that after last night, we aren't a couple?"

She held up the package. "Last night has nothing to do with this."

"Wrong."

"Damn you, Nicholas. For someone basically honorable, you can be shrewd and sly and sneaky. And for someone who speaks five languages—"

"Six, if you count Turkish."

"—you can be remarkably ambiguous."

"For a woman who's just been handed the contract of her dreams," he felt compelled to point out, "you seem remarkably reluctant to read it."

"You're trying to bribe me," she accused him in a frustrated whisper.

He figured that since she hadn't immediately torn up the papers, there was a chance she might actually, eventually, read them. "And you are afraid that if you read the offer, you'll be tempted to accept."

"Of course I'm afraid I'll accept. I've always wanted to write a book and now you've given me the perfect opportunity."

"So you're terrified your work won't be any good?"

"No."

"You're afraid you'll fail?"

"No."

"Afraid of writer's block?"

She shook her head.

"Or are you afraid of me?"

She snorted. "Don't be ridiculous."

"So what *exactly* is the problem?"

"I'm afraid I'll accept for the wrong reasons." With tears brimming once again in her eyes, she marched toward the door, clutching the contract as if it was a death sentence instead of the chance to fulfill a lifetime goal. Once again he wondered if he'd ever understand her.

Once again, she'd left him very much alone.

ERICKA WOULD NOT CRY. Tossing the unopened envelope onto her bed, she charged into her closet and tore a pantsuit off the hanger. Who the hell did he think he was? Going behind her back. Negotiating her publishing contract. Damn him. How did he know what she wanted to write?

Obviously Tashya had betrayed her confidence. Thrusting first one leg into her pants, then the other, Ericka let her fury surge through her, hoping to cleanse away her hurt and confusion. She was here to do a job, report on the coronation ceremony, and she intended to complete her assignment. She would not allow Nicholas to bribe her. She would *not* read the contract.

So then why did the plain envelope attract her like specialty chocolate wrapped in gold foil? Why did the package draw her like a hungry *Survivor* contestant to a big, juicy hamburger?

She'd never let any man come between her and success. Now was no time to start. Before, she'd always put her career first, no matter what, but already she'd agreed to delay writing the assassination story, possibly compromising her scoop. Now was not the time to let a man get under her skin, influence her decisions or orchestrate her career.

Just because they'd just shared the most passionate, exquisite sex of her lifetime. Certainly not. Just because she wanted to go back into that office and drag him over the desk and kiss him silly did not mean that she was in love.

She couldn't be in love. It had to be lust. Simple, uncomplicated lust. She could enjoy making love with Nicholas and then say goodbye with only fond memories to look back upon. So why did her insides feel as though she'd been flayed with a razor-sharp blade? Why were her hands shaking so badly she couldn't put on her shoes? And why was she having trouble seeing through the tears she wasn't going to shed?

"Ericka?" Nicholas poked his too-handsome and much-too-cocky head through the door.

She muttered the most unladylike of curses, hurled her shoe across the elegant room in his general direction. He ducked and kept advancing. "Now I know why you dyed your hair auburn—to match your hot temper."

"Get out." In no mood for his teasing, she collapsed on the satin coverlet. The envelope poked her shoulder.

Ignoring her temper, Nicholas stalked further into her room, eyes full of concern, which only increased her fury.

Yanking the package out from beneath her, she considered pitching it at him or into the trash. But she couldn't.

For one heart-stopping moment, she let her gaze lock with Nicholas' and read hope, concern and an edge of dark amusement. "Go on, open it."

"I shouldn't."

"Fine."

Bouncing onto the bed beside her, he plucked the envelope from her nerveless fingers and tugged at the tab. A stapled document slipped out and into his hands. "Usually a verbal offer is made and accepted before the publisher issues a contract, but they made an exception in your case."

"Why?" Her gaze flickered from him to the document and back, her throat tight, a bevy of hatching butterflies in her tummy.

"I thought holding a contract in your hands might make the offer more real."

Her life had changed so drastically since she'd arrived in Vashmira that nothing seemed real. Nicholas' hands, which now held her publishing contract, had skimmed over every inch of her flesh. He'd kissed her and made love to her, but that didn't give him the right to interfere in her career.

"I don't know if I'm ready to give up journalism," she told him, distracted by the fine print of the contract which called her Queen Ericka and gave her address as the palace in Vashmira.

"Your work and mine are too often at cross-purposes. If you consented to write the book—"

She scanned the document, flipping the pages. "You still might not like what I choose to put in my book."

"But the timing factor wouldn't be so critical," he told her. "After you finish the first draft, there are revisions and edits, and then it'll take another full year to come to press."

Her hands shook. "This contract is for two books—not political thrillers but biographies. One about our engagement. One about our first year of marriage." She wanted to toss the pages in his face, yet he looked so hopeful that she reconsidered. "You don't think I'll be able to cause you lots of trouble with a book? Two books?"

He grinned confidently. "Somehow, I expect you'll always be able to cause me trouble, especially if you agree to become my wife."

She dropped the contract. "We've known one another less than a week."

"Ah, but I've already learned a great deal about you," he told her with a roguish grin and proceeded to plant a simmering kiss on her earlobe.

"I can't think when you do that."

He nibbled a path down her neck. "Don't think. Say *yes*."

"To what? The contract? Making love? Keeping you?"

"How about all three?"

If she'd ever dreamed of a proposal, it wouldn't have been like this. However, as a practical career woman, she tried to consider the options and ignore her galloping pulse—and the very significant fact that he hadn't once mentioned the word *love*. "I don't even know what a queen is supposed to do."

"Your primary responsibility will be pleasuring the king," he teased.

She pushed him away. "Damn it. I'm serious."

"I know you are." He sighed and gathered her into his arms.

Resting her head on his shoulder, she relaxed against him and tried to ignore the nervous sweat on her palms. "I might embarrass you."

"Embarrassment never killed anyone. What I'm most concerned about is the danger you may be in by agreeing to marry me."

"I didn't say *yes*."

His look said he was well aware of that. "If we're going to make this marriage work, I would ask a promise from you."

Oh, no. She didn't want to make such important decisions, didn't feel ready even to hear out his request. Somehow, she dredged up the courage to look at him. And saw his pain, confusion and determination. She held her breath. "Yes?"

He made his request oh-so-casually, but she knew it had to cost him to say the words. "If you ever decide to leave me again, please, have the decency to tell me first."

"That's quite a request." She released the air in her lungs slowly. Especially since they both knew that if she warned him by declaring her intentions ahead of time, he would have the power to stop her. She didn't want to give anyone that kind of control over her. But she couldn't say no, either. Not after the passion they'd just shared. Not after he'd told her the heartbreaking story of his mother leaving his father during the middle of the revolution. He'd given her so much to think about—a new career, marriage, a new life— that her thoughts spun.

Why couldn't she drop into reporter mode? Sort the facts and make a decision? Because she couldn't catalogue her emotions so easily. However much it helped to pinpoint the problem, it didn't solve her dilemma. Right now she didn't have a clue what she wanted.

Did she love him?

Yes.

Was she willing to give up everything that had always mattered to her for him? She didn't know. Deciding the rest of her life on the spur of the moment wasn't going to happen.

He waited several tense moments for her answer, but she couldn't give him one. "I can increase the guards around you, but it cuts down on privacy. You'll have to promise me not to leave the palace without making security arrangements."

"That's not acceptable." So much for romantic proposals and everlasting promises of love. The conversation about security arrangements wasn't exactly what she'd imagined she'd be discussing immediately after receiving a proposal. "I can't—"

"You can, at least until we catch whoever is after you."

She sat up and crossed her legs. "I'm not convinced someone's after *me*." Her voice shook a little. "Steering a boat by remote control cannot be easy. The boat only aimed once in my direction. It's far more likely you are the target—just like your father was." She rolled to her side and propped her chin in her palm, considering him with a frown.

When she didn't speak, he sat up and took her hand. "What's wrong?"

"I'm starting to understand what accepting your offer entails. Living with the possibility that any moment one of your loyal subjects might step out of a crowd and shoot you."

"Our security is much improved since my father's death."

"Yeah, but all the security in the world won't do us a bit of good if the killer is someone we trust."

Chapter Eleven

After Nicholas left to attend to the growing international crisis, Ericka did what she always did when she had a personal problem. She worked.

Sitting at the desk that probably cost ten times more than her very expensive laptop, she typed all the facts she'd gathered about Nicholas' immediate family. Alexander and Tashya required several pages each, others like Sophia and the little boys only took up a paragraph. Next, Ericka sorted information on Nicholas' staff, starting with Ira Hanuck, his security chief, then moving on to General Vladimir, Peter Surak, the economic advisor, and his unpleasant wife Janna, Secretary of State Anton Belosova, his wife Natalie and daughter Larissa, and finally Ben Golden, the press secretary.

Who had the most to gain from Nicholas' demise? His brother, who would inherit the crown? The general who controlled the military? The Islamic economic advisor who feared Nicholas would admit the Jews into the country? Or Ben Golden who feared he wouldn't?

And what of Larissa Belosova? Could she have her
heart set on becoming queen? Nicholas had cut their
relationship off and her interest had turned to Alexander. Maybe she intended to pursue him and make
him king. The idea seemed far-fetched, but possible.

As Ericka considered the possibilities, she laced her
fingers together and stretched. She needed a break and
more information. These people were mostly still
strangers to her. While Nicholas had known them for
years, he might be too close to see their real motiva-
tions. She'd intended to interview each member of his
cabinet, but the crisis had made that impossible.

That left Tashya, who had gone straight to Nicholas
about Ericka's private revelation that she wanted to
write novels, and look where that had led; Sophia, who
didn't seem much interested in politics; Janna and Larissa, neither of whom seemed likely to be able to help
her. And Natalie. The wife of the secretary of state
had even offered to show her around and talk to her.

Ericka stood, strolled through her suite to the efficiency kitchen and helped herself to a cup of coffee.
Natalie seemed to have a good head on her shoulders.
She didn't excite easily and she was knowledgeable
enough for Nicholas to trust as a hostess when Tashya
or Sophia weren't available.

"Ericka," Nicholas' voice came to her from the intercom system. She walked over to it and pressed the
talk button.

"Yes?"

"Are you expecting a package from the *Washington
Herald?*" he asked, his voice tense. Her boss might

have sent over research material, background information or other related stories. However, he hadn't mentioned it during her phone conversation from Russia.

"I'm not expecting anything. Why?"

"Well, I know how you feel about me opening your mail, but I've asked Ira to—"

"You're beginning to cramp my style, Nicholas."

"Ericka."

"What?"

"The package. Ira said the package is ticking."

"What do you mean, it's ticking? Like a clock?"

"Like a bomb."

Coffee sloshed over the cup and burned her hand. "I'll be right there. Where are you?"

"The royal office. Ira has the bomb outside and the area will be cordoned off until his experts dismantle it."

She stuck her burned and shaking hand under running tap water. When the tap water did nothing to alleviate the heat, she opened the refrigerator door, found a pitcher of chilled water and poured it over her skin.

Wrapping her hand in a cool paper towel, she hurried out of her suite. Two men guarded her door. One of them followed her as she hurried toward Nicholas.

"Is everything all right, ma'am?" the guard asked her.

"Sure." Oh sure, everything was just terrific. She'd just burned her hand. The king had proposed to her without saying he loved her. Then he asked her to promise him not to leave without telling him—which effectively trapped her under his thumb. And now, his security chief was opening her mail, which happened to have a bomb inside.

Life couldn't be peachier.

ERICKA HURRIED THROUGH the guarded doors and into the royal office. Her gaze focused first on the desk, a desk that held very precious memories. But Nicholas was nowhere to be seen. She looked around the room and suddenly spied Natalie standing against the wall. Ericka could have sworn the room had been empty when she entered it, but in her rush to find Nicholas, she must have been mistaken. Natalie couldn't simply have appeared out of thin air.

The secretary of state's wife appeared startled to see her, but smoothly recovered. "If you're looking for Nicholas, he's in the courtyard." She pointed to the private garden beyond the bay window.

"Thanks. Nicholas said they found what they think is a bomb."

"I know."

"You do?"

"Anton told me on the way over. The general is sending a bomb squad. I'm glad Larissa is off with Alexander. While I'm sure the men have things under control, it's better to be safe, don't you think?"

"Actually, I'm worried about Nicholas. He isn't—"

"I assure you, he's safe, but you certainly look frazzled, dear. How about a cup of coffee? Tea?"

Ericka shook her head. She couldn't help fearing that any moment, she would hear another explosion. While she yearned to go to Nicholas and assure herself of his safety, Natalie's calm gave her pause. Natalie seemed to be a person tuned in to palace politics; perhaps she would learn more by staying here. "On second thought, I'd love a cup of tea."

Natalie used the intercom to have tea brought to them, obviously comfortable in Nicholas' office. She wore a stunning dark pantsuit, sandals and a lovely silk scarf fastened with a brooch.

"I take it you've been here a lot?" Ericka asked as she sank into one of the plush antique chairs positioned around a coffee table, thinking it would be rude to ask the woman why she was here, so she hoped she'd volunteer the information.

She didn't. Composed and relaxed, Natalie sat in the opposite chair, crossing one elegant leg over the other. Totally in control and comfortable in social situations, Natalie appeared to be the perfect wife for a secretary of state. "Anton and Zared I were good friends for over thirty years. Back in the old days, the men planned the revolution around my kitchen table, and we all ate fish Anton had caught that morning."

"Do you know any more about the bomb?" Ericka asked, knowing she wouldn't relax until she had all the details.

"Actually, I do, since I overheard Anton and the general. The package addressed to you is tied with string and the address is handwritten."

"Nicholas said it's ticking."

"Don't worry. The men have detection devices. And a portable X-ray system. I'm surprised you're so interested—"

"Why would I not be?"

"Ah, our tea. Set it right here and I'll pour," Natalie directed the servant. "I thought you would be more interested in the coronation.'' Natalie poured and handed her a steaming cup of green tea.

Ericka helped herself to a slice of lemon and two sugar cubes. ''Correspondents are often sent to cover one story and find themselves on another.''

''Ah, but the pomp and ceremony of the coronation, the sheer romanticism of Nicholas becoming our king sort of grabs a woman's heart, don't you think?''

''Tell me more,'' Ericka suggested. She assumed that Natalie could tell her no more about the bomb, but the woman clearly wanted to talk about the Vash-miran society event of the decade.

''You must understand our history to comprehend the events about to take place. This is the land of Spartacus, which belonged to the kingdom of Macedonia. By 46 B.C. the Romans had conquered the area.''

''Whoa.'' Ericka didn't want a two-thousand-year history lesson. ''Why don't you tell me about the royal family. My editor only wants relatively recent news. Say the last twenty years?''

''After Zared's revolution succeeded,'' Natalie switched gears without effort, ''our people had unrealistic expectations. At first abrupt curtailments of trade with the Soviet bloc brought about hardships. Our people have had to readjust. Twenty years ago, we had no checking accounts, credit cards or ATM machines. We had to catch up. Some of our people missed the old social benefits like guaranteed employment, free nurseries, higher education and medical care. Lack of resources set our differing factions at odds with each other.''

''But you never returned to communism?'' Ericka

asked, knowing the answer, but curious how Natalie interpreted her past.

"Not like Lithuania, Poland, Bulgaria and Hungary. We stayed a democratic monarchy, thanks to Zared I." Her voice turned proud. "Vashmira is a prospective member of the European Union, and we are now considered 'investment grade' by international grading companies."

"But?"

"We paid a price for the painful economic restructuring. Unemployment was very high and inflation almost went out of control before Peter Surak, our economic advisor, got a handle on it. Through it all, our people stuck together. We had internal squabbles, but no fighting. Now, we will show our success to the world with a peaceful transition of power from father to son. And Nicholas will announce your engagement," Natalie leaned forward. "I'm so pleased."

"Would you have preferred he'd chosen Larissa?" Ericka asked and watched Natalie's eyes carefully.

The woman met hers with no embarrassment. "Nothing would have made me happier," she admitted. "But it's not to be, I'm afraid. Larissa seems to prefer Alexander."

"You don't approve?"

"Alexander is a notorious playboy. I fear in the end, my daughter will be hurt."

Natalie seemed no more, no less, than a concerned mother. And while Ericka assumed she was hiding some secrets, she didn't dig further.

"Tell me about Janna and Peter Surak," she requested, instead.

"I have nothing but respect for Peter. He's a financial genius. Educated at Eton. From a fine Muslim family. He works hard, but I've often thought he works so hard to escape from his home life. You've met Janna..."

"Is there a reason she is so bitter?"

"Janna loved Zared I."

"Really?"

"He was charming to all the women, but he wanted nothing to do with her. However, I don't think that made her into the shrew she is today.... Please don't quote me?"

"Okay."

"Her husband cannot have children. An old war injury, I believe."

Had Janna's bitterness turned her into a killer? Ericka didn't know, but she vowed to learn the woman's whereabouts the day the boat exploded on the beach.

"How long has Ben Golden worked for Nicholas?"

"Our Jewish press secretary? Would you believe he won a scholarship to Eton and the Jew and Peter, a Muslim, became best friends? Peter recommended Ben for the position several years ago."

"Ben's single?"

"As is our general. Although the general keeps a mistress." Natalie gave the information with a smug smile, almost as if she approved. Possibly she was just pleased she could impart gossip.

"And Sophia? Her year of mourning is almost over. Will she marry again?"

"If you're asking me if the woman truly loved Zared I, my answer is an unequivocal *yes*. She adored him. She would have done anything for him, given him ten children if he asked it of her. Whether another man can ever fill the void in her heart? That I do not know.''

''You certainly are well informed.''

''I thought since you're soon to become one of us it would help if I filled you in. Tashya is a fine girl, but she's oblivious to gossip.''

''Really? How does she spend her time?''

''With her horses.'' Natalie wrinkled her nose. ''She often smells like a stable hand. I've never understood why she can't leave the care of her animals to servants.''

''I take it you're not a horse lover.''

''Afraid not.''

''But Larissa rides.''

''Her father insisted she take lessons so she could go on the royal outings. She fills in as hostess when I'm committed elsewhere.''

A servant entered and handed Ericka a note from Nicholas. ''Come to the courtyard. You'll want to see this.''

NICHOLAS CLUTCHED THE device in his hand, barely noticing the pain as the sharp edges of metal bit into his palm. He simply waited for Ericka to find him in the courtyard, knowing she needed to hear a full explanation—even if she left him now that they knew her life was truly in danger.

''Nicholas, what's wrong?'' Her guard trailing her footsteps, Ericka hurried to him, her face full of concern, her gaze scanning the courtyard for danger.

He led her to a bench beside a marble fountain with a statue of Hercules at the center. After they both sat, he gathered his thoughts. "I suppose I should start at the beginning."

"When our fathers made our marriage contract?"

"Earlier than that. In fact, my story starts shortly after your birth."

He took her hand, and she scooted closer to him but turned so she could watch his face. "During the revolution, my father, your father and General Vladimir often shared a foxhole. Since they often spent the nights planning the next day's battles, other men performed the chore of digging for them."

"One rainy morning, the trio found themselves pinned by especially heavy mortar fire. Your father took a bullet in the fleshy part of his arm."

"He died from a superficial wound that became infected?" Ericka guessed. Obviously her mother hadn't known or hadn't told her the details of her father's death.

"His wound was not life threatening, but knocked him deep into the hole. He landed face downward in the wet mud. And between the hail of bullets, the thunder of mortar fire and the rain, he must have heard an odd ticking."

"A bomb?"

"He didn't know. Ignoring his wound, he took off his helmet and used it to dig into the mud. The general and my father continued to shoot back at the enemy, unaware of the problem below their feet."

"Damn. He found a bomb, didn't he?"

"Apparently he uncovered the mechanism a mere

second before detonation. He had no time to dislodge it or pitch it out of the foxhole. He fell on it, used his own body to protect the others. Due to his actions and the soaking from torrential rains, the gunpowder only partially detonated.''

''He didn't die right away, did he?''

''My father wrote some of this to you, but I never knew exactly what he said,'' Nicholas gently told her.

''He said my father died protecting his back.''

''He did.''

''And then they made our marriage contract, so my father must have lived for at least a little while afterward.'' She paled and her hand trembled in his.

Nicholas didn't tell her it had taken several excruciating hours for her father to die. There had been no morphine, not even for Zared's best friend. He cleared his throat and continued. ''The bomb was Russian made, the timepiece dented from your father's heroics. The general kept the timepiece—first to try and trace the serial numbers, but he failed. Later I suppose it became a souvenir.''

She quickly regained control of her emotions, morphing into reporter mode. ''Nicholas, why are you now telling me about the past?''

''Because of this.'' He opened his hand and showed her a twisted bit of brass.

''What is it?''

''It's the timer from the bomb that took your father's life.''

''But you said the general kept it.''

''We found this in the bomb sent to you, supposedly from your editor at the *Washington Herald*.''

"I don't understand."

"Neither do I. Ira dusted the parcel's wrapping paper for prints. The general's weren't on the package."

"He could have worn gloves."

"Actually, there were no prints at all on the paper, which is odd, since it had to have been handled by postal workers."

"Maybe it wasn't," she said. "Diplomatic and military mail comes through in special pouches," Ericka suggested, "which isn't leaving us much to go on—just like the boat explosion which burned up the pieces at such a high temperature that Ira had no clues to track down."

"This time we have one." Nicholas tossed the timer into the air and caught it, closing his fingers fiercely. "The general has some explaining to do."

"Is he in the palace?" Ericka asked.

"Why? You want to question him?"

"Absolutely."

At her answer, relief washed through him along with more worry. "I thought…"

"What?"

"You might…want to leave."

She lifted her chin, her determination warriorlike. "If I left, I'd never find the man who murdered my father."

"Okay." He'd been hoping she'd stay for him. But he could understand her need to track down her father's killer. How could he not after he'd spent the last year doing exactly the same thing?

"However, a lot of this puzzle doesn't make sense," she went on, completely oblivious to how much he wanted her to let him handle the investigation while she stayed out of the line of fire, safely guarded. But he knew better than to insist.

"In what way?"

"It would make sense to assume the same person was responsible for the bomb in that foxhole and the bomb sent to me. But…" She frowned as she worked through the details. "The general wouldn't have set a bomb in his own foxhole."

"Unless he'd planned to make an excuse to leave and couldn't because of the heavy shelling."

"And why would he use a timer traceable to him?" Ericka shook her head. "He has access to parts from an entire arsenal. No doubt, he'd know you'd recognize that particular part—"

"Not if Ira's men hadn't disarmed the bomb, we wouldn't. The timer would have been blown to bits."

"Well," she looked at him. "I'm up for talking to the general. Why don't we surprise him with an unexpected visit?"

When he didn't reply immediately, she sighed. "What?"

"I have to ask."

"I'm not staying in the palace." Already she knew him well enough to guess his thoughts. Her words were soft but forceful. "Forget it. I'm the one who grew up without a father. And apparently, it's my life at stake."

They both stood, and he took her into his arms. Strong, powerful arms that held her with tenderness and promise. "Your life means a lot to me."

"Yeah, I know. If we don't marry, Vashmira will—"

"I meant to me—personally."

"Oh."

"In fact, despite having to face your temper, I'm considering sending you someplace safe—"

"*No.* You speak five, make that six languages. You do know the meaning of the word?"

He held her closer, close enough to feel his heartbeat, close enough for her to feel his warmth. "I should send you someplace where no one can hurt you, no matter how much you protest."

She looked at him without pulling away. Instead, she stroked his shoulder soothingly. "Nicholas, we've been through this before. I could be attacked anywhere, even here in the palace."

Like his father.

She snuggled against his chest. "Actually, the safest place is next to you and your contingent of guards."

"You have a point."

"And I like going with you."

"Enough to marry me?" he asked, his confidence blooming with every word she spoke.

She winked at him. "I'm considering your request." She slipped her hands around his neck and tugged his head down. "How about trying to convince me with another kiss?"

ERICKA BREATHED IN HIS kiss like a drowning woman starved for oxygen. She plastered herself against him, parlaying a stolen second into a treasure trove of sparkling moments. And just like every other time she had touched him, she wanted more, more than lust, more than a quick kiss.

When he finally pulled back, his eyes resembled hot blue sparks, sparks she wanted to set aflame. However, much as she yearned to pursue her growing feelings, now was not the time.

Still, the heat of his kiss kept the edge off her impatience during the short car ride to the general's house. Set in an established but modest neighborhood, the one-story log home had a steeply pitched roof, a smoking chimney and a front porch, and it was shaded by fir trees. It appeared to be the home of a family man—not a bachelor. Purple and white flowers grew in window boxes, and the lush green lawn was well tended, the sidewalks and driveway newly edged.

"You've been here before?" she asked Nicholas.

"Never without an invitation." A restless energy manifested his distress. "I'd like you to ask most of the questions, as if you're doing an interview."

"Sure," she agreed, albeit wondering about his reasons, wondering if he feared losing control. Clearly, Nicholas was troubled, revealing how deeply he cared, but about whom and what? Were his emotions set on high due to his still unspoken feelings for her and her safety? Or were his emotions due to feelings of betrayal by his father's old friend?

Clearly, he intended to keep his emotions in check. She supposed he didn't want to insult an ally—in case they were wrong.

The general opened the door with composure and escorted Nicholas, Ericka and four guards into his study.

His father's old friend didn't reveal surprise at Nicholas' appearance nor did Ericka expect him to. From everything she knew about the cagey warrior who had won many battles, both military and political, he didn't panic. The ultimate survivor, he'd escaped the Russian system and thrived in Vashmira. Ericka had already noted that age had not dulled his sensory antennae and in his mid-fifties, the general was in the prime of his life.

His simple study smelled of lemon wax and pipe smoke. The general offered them drinks, which they declined, then seats beside his fireplace. Two guards came inside and stood protectively at the door, the others waited outside the door. Ericka looked around curiously and, recalling Nicholas' request, took out a pen and pad of paper from her purse.

The general threw back his head and swallowed a shot of vodka and spoke to Nicholas in his strong Russian accent. "To what do I owe the pleasure, my friend?"

"I was telling Ericka about her father's brave death and his sacrifice. She's asked to see the timer from the bomb her father threw himself upon. And she wants to ask you a few questions."

The general's eyes settled on Ericka, sizing her up. "I will make it a gift to you."

He stood stiffly, marched to a shelf full of military hardware that included a pineapple grenade casing, a samurai sword and several pistols. Nicholas had told her on the way over that the mementos in this room all held personal memories for the general.

The general frowned at the shelf. "The timer is not here."

"When was the last time you saw it?" Ericka asked casually, but suspected he read her concern. The wily Russian had a vigilant nature, always scanning his surroundings, alert to what was awry, out of place or dangerous—especially in his dealings with other people. Nicholas had told her the man also liked to keep his own counsel and rarely asked for outside opinions or advice. He made decisions easily and took care of himself.

"A month ago, maybe two, was when I last handled the timer. I am not sure."

"You cannot remember?" Nicholas asked.

The general shrugged. "It's not a valuable item to anyone but those of us who hold memories of the past close to our hearts."

"I'd like a list of everyone who has been in your house since then." Nicholas framed his words as a request but everyone recognized the order.

"May I ask why?"

"The timer turned up inside a package addressed and sent to Ericka. We found and disarmed a live bomb inside. The timer had the same serial number as the one on your shelf."

The general grimaced, kept pacing. "Someone went to a lot of trouble to set me up."

Ericka kept her tone calm. "Or maybe you sent it?"

"Young woman, if I wanted you dead, I could have thought of fifty, no, a hundred ways to accomplish it with no clues that would lead back to me. I have an entire army at my disposal, including some of the former Soviet Union's elite fighting troops.''

Every word the general spoke was true. Ericka had no doubt he could pull off a covert assassination without leaving a clue that would lead straight back to him.

The general poured himself another shot of vodka then paced. ''The list is a short one. The lady who comes to clean. The man who delivers my groceries. Both are villagers.''

''That's it?'' Ericka asked boldly, recalling her conversation with Natalie about his mistress, then realized the delicate nature of this interview. The general was one of the most powerful men in Vashmira. With trouble on the border, Nicholas needed his goodwill, his respect and his expertise. No wonder he'd suggested she ask the hard questions.

Nicholas depended on General Vladimir just as his father had. He didn't want to insult the man unnecessarily, especially when he'd never given any reason for his loyalty to be doubted. Until now.

''Perhaps a stranger picked my lock and stole the timer,'' the general suggested.

''Perhaps,'' Nicholas replied, his tone neutral.

''*No one* else has been here?'' Ericka pressed him.

''There was…someone…another woman,'' the general admitted.

''Your mistress?'' Ericka asked. ''Who is she?''

''She's a married woman.'' Vladimir looked longingly at the vodka, then shook his head. Ericka imagined that the general's loyalties were torn between duty to Nicholas and devotion to his lady. Perhaps he might loosen up if she came at him from a different angle.

"How long have you known her?" Ericka asked.

"Thirty-five years. Long enough to know she doesn't have the knowledge to use that timer in a bomb."

"But she knew the timer's history?" Ericka pressed.

The general nodded. His pacing ceased in front of Nicholas. "Do you wish my resignation?"

"No." Nicholas stood and faced his father's old friend, who kept his back military straight, his demeanor strong and proud. "I wish the lady's name."

"There is no other way?" the general asked him.

"None." Nicholas clapped the general on the shoulder. "I promise you that we will question her without her husband's knowledge."

"Her husband knows. It's her child…"

Ericka's jaw dropped. "What kind of man allows his wife to have an affair with another for, for…"

"Three decades," the general filled in for her, and she swallowed a gasp. "I have asked myself that many times. What kind of man am I to settle for a mistress when I wanted her for a wife?"

Ericka now had the reason why the general had never married. He loved his married mistress. No wonder he didn't want to reveal her identity. However, she had to insist.

"Sir, maybe she innocently gave the timer to another. Maybe she had no intention of doing harm. We will investigate and find the truth. But I must have her name because someone is trying to kill me, and if we don't figure out their identity soon, they may very well succeed.''

"Please, ask the guards to leave," the general requested of Nicholas, pain in his eyes, anguish in his voice.

Nicholas, cords in his neck tight, nodded for the guards to go. One thrust a pistol into his hands. "Sir, if we're going to leave you alone with him, you should be armed."

Nicholas placed the gun across his lap with a casual ease that indicated his familiarity with firearms. But no gesture could release the stress of waiting to hear the general's next words. She had no doubt that beyond his mostly unruffled exterior Nicholas' fury burned hot and deep. Yet, he would withhold judgment, wait for answers, and she could only respect his self-control.

"Fine. Fine." The general waved them out the door. "Just go."

Nicholas waited in silence until the door snapped shut. The logs in the burning fireplace crackled as if manifesting his tension.

Ericka refused to allow any more delay. Even as they spoke, the woman could be escaping or hatching another diabolical plan. "Your mistress' name, General?''

"Natalie. Natalie Belosova.''

Chapter Twelve

On the drive back to the palace with Nicholas, Ericka recalled her conversation with the wife of the secretary of state, wondering if she'd missed hints or clues. "Natalie told me that the general had a mistress. At the time, I thought she sounded smug because she was pleased to be in the know about palace gossip, but I never dreamed she was talking about herself."

Nicholas shrugged. "She's fooled many people. Who would think proper, respectable Natalie would have an affair for thirty years or that her husband knows about it?"

"She doesn't seem the type," Ericka agreed, "not the least bit flirtatious, but oh-so-proper."

"With a husband and a lover, why would she flirt with other men?" Nicholas pointed out.

Ericka recalled how stunned she'd been by the general's revelation and how unruffled Nicholas had appeared. "You knew about Natalie's long-term affair with the general didn't you?"

"Yes. It's my duty to know about the people I work with. I couldn't very well allow the general to risk being blackmailed by our enemies to keep his affair secret. But since Anton knows,'' Nicholas shrugged, ''I figured it was none of my business.''

''It becomes your business if Natalie sent the bomb and if she could also be the one who assassinated your father,'' Ericka said. ''While she had means and opportunity—don't forget she was also at the beach the day of the boat bomb—what's her motive?''

''I always thought she liked my father. Actually, she doted on him.''

Ericka frowned at Nicholas, trying to work out the puzzle. ''Natalie told me your father was charming. You think she loved Anton, the general and your father?''

''Sounds far-fetched, doesn't it?''

Ericka searched for a motive for murder that made sense. ''Do you think it's possible that Natalie became obsessed with the thought of Larissa becoming queen?''

Nicholas raised an eyebrow. ''So she decided to kill off the competition—namely you?''

''Mothers do strange things for their children. In Texas, a mother was convicted of plotting murder to help her daughter make the cheerleading squad.''

''She plotted to kill a child?''

''Actually she went after the child's mother. Apparently she thought the girl would be so upset over her mother's death that she wouldn't make the team. And this was a woman with no record. She seemed totally normal until then.''

''Like Natalie.''

Ericka leaned against Nicholas and sighed.

"We should have answers soon," Nicholas told her. "Natalie's at the palace, and I've asked my guards to bring her to my office for questioning."

"What about her husband?"

Nicholas shook his head. "I want to question them separately, but we'll have to wait for answers from my secretary of state. Anton secretly flew out last night to meet with a joint Israeli-American-Russian delegation."

"Are they close to a solution?" Ericka asked. She'd almost forgotten the tense situation on the border and wondered how Nicholas juggled so many different concerns. For his sake and the sake of the refugees waiting on the border, she hoped that the demonstrations in the streets and the entire episode could end peacefully before the coronation ceremony.

"Anton's working on it."

When they arrived at the palace, Ira met them at the gate. "Sir, we cannot find Mrs. Belosova."

Beside her Nicholas tensed, his voice hardened. "Place additional guards around Ms. Allen. She is not to go anywhere alone until we locate and detain Natalie."

"Yes, Your Highness."

Ericka didn't protest. In truth, she'd be grateful for the extra protection. "I thought Natalie was here at the palace?"

"She checked in," Ira informed them as they walked toward Ericka's private quarters, "an hour ago. We've combed the grounds and the public areas, and we've done a complete sweep of the suites. We haven't located her yet."

"She didn't check out?" Nicholas asked.

"No, Your Majesty."

An aide hustled around a corner and veered straight for Nicholas. "Your Highness, you've an urgent phone call from the secretary of state. Negotiations are breaking down."

Nicholas nodded. "I'll take the call in my office. Ask him to hold."

He turned to Ericka, calm, his eyes dark with worry. He removed from his jacket pocket the gun that the guards had given him earlier at the general's house and pressed it into her hand. "Do you know how to use this?"

Her mouth went dry. "No."

"Ira, give her a quick lesson. Post guards around her quarters, doors and windows. I want her safe."

"Yes, Your Highness."

Nicholas pulled her close for an embrace and kissed her hard on the mouth, tension in every muscle of his body. "I'll come to you as soon as I can."

Before she could even relax against him, he released her, leaving her very alone, her heart beating much too quickly. He headed toward his office, and she had the horrible feeling she might never see him again.

Get a grip. She'd never had a premonition that had come true in her entire life. Nicholas would be fine and so would she.

Ira gently took the gun from her hand. He flicked a little switch on the gun. "This is the safety. I've released it. That means if you pull the trigger, the gun will fire. You have six bullets."

"Shouldn't we put the safety back on?" Ericka asked.

The fierce man spoke gently. "I don't want you fumbling with an unfamiliar weapon at a crucial time. All you need to do, is identify your target, point and shoot."

He offered her the gun, and she took it reluctantly, careful not to touch the trigger. As if sensing her distaste, he assured her, "It's only a precaution. We'll search your suite top to bottom before we let you go in. After you're safely inside, my men will guard the perimeter. We'll be within shouting distance at every moment. You'll be fine."

She didn't feel fine. Natalie might be trying to kill her. Natalie, who knew the layout of the palace as well as Nicholas. The woman had already made one trip to Ericka's suite. Had she been there to check out the layout before Ericka returned? Or perhaps Natalie had already planted another bomb there?

"Ira, I'd like to pick up my computer and then work in Nicholas' quarters. Why go where—"

"Natalie expects to find you?"

"Exactly," she said with more determination than she felt. The tension raked her until she wanted to hit someone, run somewhere, scream. But there was no enemy to strike or evade.

Every minute she waited to enter her suite while Ira's men searched seemed like days. Finally, they allowed her to enter. She gathered up a notebook and her laptop and the still unopened publishing contract. Minutes later, they performed another time-consuming search of Nicholas' quarters before finally allowing her to go inside.

Placing her laptop on a desk, she plugged it in, hoping work would take her mind off the waiting. The publishing contract called to her and she picked it up, then read it.

Excitement and fear warred with each other. On one hand she wanted to call her boss, drink champagne and celebrate. On the other, she trembled at the huge task of writing an entire book. Two books. Up until now, she'd only written newspaper articles. A book was a different animal, complex, with plots and characters and twists and turns. She should be eager to start.

The advance with its six zeros was enough to assure her financial security for the rest of her life, even if she never sold another book. And suddenly she realized that while this money had been her ultimate goal, it represented much more than the ability to purchase whatever she liked. The money allowed her the freedom to choose how she worked, where she worked, or if she worked ever again. Marrying Nicholas and spending his money wouldn't be the same as earning her own way. If she accepted, this contract would give her choices she'd never expected to have.

So why did she feel as if Nicholas had pulled the rug out from under her? He'd helped to make her independently wealthy. She should be delighted about reaching a long-term goal much, much sooner than she'd ever expected.

Now that the opportunity was in her hands, she

should be dancing. Instead she felt a huge sob welling up in her chest.

Idiot.

She felt as if she were mourning the person she had once been—and not quite ready to tackle the difficult job of growing into the woman she would become. That she loved Nicholas she had no doubt—but was that enough? She could give up her journalism career and write these books—but then what? She'd always had something to strive for and now she felt at a loss. She had no idea what she wanted and felt like a fool.

Any sane woman would be ecstatic about marrying Nicholas, even if he weren't the king. Yet, contemplating marriage to him, becoming a queen, took courage she wasn't sure she had. She had no clue as to what her new life would be like. Suppose she failed at it? Suppose she hated it?

Until now, she'd only been responsible for herself. If she accepted Nicholas' proposal, she would be included in a large family, his inner circle, his kingdom. She didn't suppose she could buy a book on the *Idiot's Guide to Being a Queen.*

And yet, what could be a greater challenge than helping Nicholas? From what she'd seen of this country so far, there was so much work to be done, she could choose her own direction. The thought was both scary and exhilarating.

She wanted children someday and Nicholas already doted on his little brothers. He'd be a wonderful father. Possibilities opened before her and she realized she had nothing to fear. Changes were scary, but they could be good changes.

She'd have to think about her future some more, give the numerous possibilities much more consideration, but right now, she needed to complete her current assignment. Needed to write down her thoughts about the meeting with the general. Besides, she knew no better way to settle her mind than to work.

She placed the gun next to her on the desk within easy reach and opened her computer screen.

She tapped a key and a message flashed across the screen.

She leaned forward. Neatly typed black words practically shouted at her.

Leave Vashmira within the hour and never return. Say nothing to anyone. Fail to heed any part of my demand and Nicholas will die.

The threat to Nicholas scared her enough to sap the strength from her legs. Sagging into a chair, she reread the demand, wondering who'd had access to her laptop while she'd been gone.

Ericka might have encountered danger many times in her career, but worrying over Nicholas' safety knocked her normal strength right out of her. As if in a nightmare, she read the demand again, hoping, praying, that this time the words would be different. Of, course they weren't. Nicholas had a traitor in his midst. One who boldly entered the palace at will. Her fear for Nicholas escalated as she realized how easily the assassin had murdered his father. Despite increased palace security, could the same killer get to Nicholas?

She should gather her things. Leave. Leave without

saying one word to Nicholas, who would undoubtably try to stop her. She should go. Now.

Don't panic.

Natalie Belosova wouldn't evade the palace security teams for long. She'd be brought in for questioning.

But Natalie could be innocent. The general had named two villagers who also had had access to his home. However, only Natalie had known the history of the timer, been on the beach the day the boat exploded and had free rein of the palace grounds.

Sure, eventually security would catch her. Ice seemed to replace the blood in Ericka's veins while her mind whirled with suspicions. Was Natalie working alone? Could there be a conspiracy?

Ericka shivered, yanked the coverlet from Nicholas' bed and dragged it over her shoulders. Rocking, she hugged herself, thinking she should go. Nicholas meant so much to her. She would never forgive herself if she selfishly stayed and her actions put him in danger. She could sacrifice spending a lifetime with him if her actions would save his life.

Oh, hell.

If she abandoned Nicholas, he would see her action as the ultimate betrayal. He would think of her as he did his mother, as a coward, a foreigner, a traitor. He'd curse her soul to the end of his days. Nicholas had many great qualities, but she sensed he wouldn't ever forget or forgive the kind of betrayal she was considering—especially since asking her to talk to him before she left had been the only request he'd made of her. If she sneaked away like a thief in the night, she'd slice his pride to shreds, destroy his faith in her. Yet, she'd prefer his hating her to his death.

But that was her preference. She knew—because he had told her so—that he would prefer to make the decision himself. Was it wrong of her to take the decision away from him?

Yes.

What the hell was she going to do? Stay and risk his life? Or go and betray the man she loved?

Damn. She should pack. Leave him before he returned. She couldn't maintain a stoic front as he could. He'd take one look into her eyes and see her pain, realize she was seriously considering something drastic, like whether or not to flee.

Didn't he have the right to decide whether to risk his own life? And suddenly she realized how much she loved him—enough to honor his wishes—enough to allow him to risk his life—even if she preferred otherwise.

She'd thought leaving the man she loved would be the hardest thing she'd ever done, but she was wrong. Staying would be oh-so-much more difficult. Terrifyingly difficult. Every moment she would fear for his safety. Every time they were together, she'd fear it could be their last. If she stayed, she'd have to live every minute knowing that if she'd complied with the anonymous demand she could have kept Nicholas safe.

Did she love him enough to allow him to risk his life? The question tore at her heart, ripped at her soul. She'd lost her father and her mother. She knew the pain of loving and losing those she loved, didn't know where she would find the courage to stay and watch Nicholas fight for his life—but she would find that bravery—or she would fake it.

Heart aching but the decision made, Ericka calmly glanced at her laptop's screen again. Maybe Ira could dust the keypad for fingerprints.

Ericka slapped the desk and stood, then heard an odd thud from the direction of the far bedroom wall where heavy draperies hung. She turned and saw a drape flutter and a musty breeze wafted across the room. She told herself an open window was the cause of the sudden breeze, but the draperied wall didn't face a courtyard or outer wall and served as mere decoration.

The curtain fluttered again.

Determined, fear slicing her stomach like barbwire, Ericka hauled up the gun and pointed it at the drapes.

And heard a high-pitched laugh.

Chapter Thirteen

"Nicholas?" The immature voice floated across the room on a stream of wind.

Ericka continued to aim the gun at the rippling drapes. Someone had sneaked behind them, but why hadn't palace security noticed?

A chill swept over her as she considered whether someone on the security team had deliberately missed checking behind the drapes. If she called out, would help come?

"Nicholas. Where are you?" The high-pitched voice from behind the curtains sounded feminine and eerie.

Ericka considered fleeing from the room, but this might be the best chance to stop whoever was after her. Were they calling for Nicholas because it was his room?

Torn between screaming for the guards and keeping quiet to surprise the prowler, Ericka held her breath, remaining silent and still. She didn't know whether to hope the assassin was about to come out from behind the draperies or not. Didn't know whether she could pull the trigger or not.

A hand lifted the drape. A very tiny hand. The hand of a woman, perhaps. Or a child.

"Uncle Nicholas?"

"Dimitri?"

No assassin, just Nicholas' little brother, slowly emerged, first his feet, then his dirty coveralls.

With a sigh of relief and frustration, Ericka lowered the gun, flicked on the safety and set the weapon on top of a six-foot-tall dresser where the mischievous boys couldn't possibly reach it.

By the time she turned back, Dimitri had lifted the bottom of the heavy drape for Nikita and then the two boys crawled into the room and stood up. Sticky cobwebs in their hair, their white teeth shining through the dust and grime on their faces, both children grinned at her. She didn't know whether to kiss them or scold them.

Dimitri held a flashlight in one hand and took his brother's hand with the other. "I told you we could find Nicholas' rooms."

"We did it," Nikita agreed. "Where's Nicholas?"

"He's working," Ericka answered, confounded by their appearance. How had they evaded their mother and palace security? "How did you two guys get in here?"

"Shh." Dimitri flicked off the flashlight and set it down by his feet, then straightened and lifted a filthy finger to his dusty lips. "It's a secret."

Heart still pounding, Ericka hurried to the wall and

lifted the thick material of the drapes. Beyond the pan-
eled wall lay a dark passageway. A secret tunnel.

She'd be willing to bet her entire advance that Zared's assassin had used a similar tunnel to get away
from the royal office. There might be an entire laby-
rinth of passages—especially if the kids had traveled
from Sophia's quarters all the way to Nicholas'.

And that person had used the same passages to plant
the note in her room and leave undetected. Somehow
the secret corridors had to have been concealed for
years, maybe centuries, or Nicholas certainly would
have known about them. "How do you go in and
out?"

Dimitri leaned over and tripped a tiny lever set between two wooden panels. The opening silently slid
shut. "Neat, huh?"

The wall now appeared solid. Looking at the wall,
no one would have guessed what lay behind it.

While her mind spun with theories, Ericka took both
boys by the hand and led them toward the bathroom.
"How did you guys get in there?"

"There's lots of secret doors. Once you know the
secret, finding them is easy. The hard part is not getting lost," Dimitri told her.

Ericka sighed, glad the two boys had traveled
through the dark passages unharmed. "Somehow, I
think Sophia might be looking for you two."

"She's not," Nikita said, frowning as Ericka took
a clean hand towel off the rack, wet it under the running faucet and wrung it out.

Kneeling, she wiped Nikita's face clean, then used

the other side on Dimitri. "Why isn't your mom looking for you?"

"She thinks we're sleeping," Dimitri told her. "We need to go back before she figures out—"

"No way am I letting you two disappear inside that dark passage," Ericka told them.

"But—" Dimitri protested.

Ericka reached over to an intercom. "Can someone connect me to Sophia, please?"

The intercom clicked and a moment later Ericka heard Sophia's soft, sleepy voice. "Yes?"

"This is Ericka Allen. Your sons have come to visit me again."

"Again? They are supposed to be sleeping." Sophia sounded as if she'd been taking a nap herself. "How did they evade their guards?"

"I'll show you when you arrive. I'm in Nicholas' suite. Could you please bring him with you, too?"

"I'll try. And don't let those rascals out of your sight."

"Uh oh." Nikita's bottom lip quivered. "She sounded mad."

"Are we in trouble?" Dimitri asked Ericka.

"What do you think?" Ericka led the boys back into the bedroom, sat in a chair and pulled both of them onto her lap. "Suppose you got stuck between the walls and nobody knew where you were?"

"The tunnels are too big to get stuck."

"Suppose you got lost?"

Dimitri shoved his hands into his pockets and dribbled crumbs onto the floor. "I dropped crackers, so we could find our way back."

"That was smart, but suppose a cat or a bug ate your crackers? Then you would have been lost, and we wouldn't have been able to find you."

"We could have banged on the walls." Dimitri had an answer for everything. He was a bright, resourceful kid, but he had to be made to understand that he couldn't go off exploring on his own.

"Dimitri, this palace is very big. You might have pounded on the walls for a very long time before we found you. Promise me that the next time you guys go exploring, you'll take a guard with you."

"They ruin all the fun," Nikita complained.

"They'll keep you safe."

Sophia rushed into the apartment with Nicholas several steps behind her. Sophia took one look at the boys and sighed. "You will take both a shower and a bath tonight."

"Ah, mother."

"Don't you 'ah, mother' me, young man. You've gone too far this time."

"We stayed right inside the palace," Dimitri argued.

Sophia nodded at Ericka. "Thank you for finding them."

"Actually they found me." Ericka pulled back the heavy drape. "Go on, Dimitri. Show your Uncle Nicholas how you sneaked past all his guards."

The child pressed the lever, and the panel whisked open. Air and dust blew into the room. "Cool, huh?"

Nicholas patted the child on the head and exchanged a long look with Ericka over the significance of the passageway. "You may have just solved a huge mystery."

"Is that good or bad?" Dimitri asked.

At his question, Sophia, Ericka and Nicholas chuckled.

Dimitri rolled his eyes at the odd behavior of the adults and took his brother's hand. Sophia departed with the kids, leaving Nicholas and Ericka alone.

Nicholas frowned at the opening and called his guards.

Two uniformed men rushed into his suite. Nicholas drew back the drape and pointed to the tunnel. "You two guard this entrance. And be on the lookout for others that lead into my quarters."

"Yes, Your Majesty."

"Have the chief talk to my brothers about the secret entrances and send men to flush out Natalie Belosova. I want her alive."

"Yes, Your Highness."

MINUTES LATER, NICHOLAS received a message from Ira through the intercom system. "Your Majesty, we've cornered Natalie. She's standing on the tower and threatening to jump unless you come and speak to her."

"I'll be right there."

"I'm coming with you," Ericka told him. Even though she realized she still had smudges of dirt on her face from holding the children, she wasn't going to let that stop her. "Where and what is the tower?"

He took her hand, and they sprinted down several long corridors. Surprised servants and busy aides jumped out of the way. "The tower is a circular structure that was once manned by sentinels and overlooks the outer bailey. That part of the palace hasn't been renovated in the last thousand years."

Ericka matched his long stride. "Natalie must have figured she wouldn't be found there."

"The walls are crumbling. When we arrive, you will watch your step. Stay back."

"Yes, Your Majesty. I'll be just as careful as you are."

There was no sarcasm in her tone this time, just concern. Obviously she worried over his safety as much as he worried over hers. Instead of feeling annoyance the thought warmed him.

Nicholas led Ericka outside and then up a crumbling stairwell probably built by Crusaders. Breathing hard, they reached the tower to find Natalie standing precariously inside a turret, her body flattened into a crenel, a spot from where archers once shot flaming arrows, her signature white hair flying loose around her drawn face.

Ira stepped forward. "We believe she's unarmed, Your Highness, but I would advise that you go no closer."

Nicholas nodded and shouted. "I'm here, Natalie. No one will hurt you. You can come down, now."

Natalie leaned out over the bailey far below with a perilous disregard for her life. "Anton and Larissa had no part in my actions. I never meant to hurt anyone."

"Of course, you didn't. Come down so we can all talk," Nicholas told her.

Natalie didn't budge, except to shake her head.

Nicholas noted she'd kicked off her shoes and gripped the stones with her fingers and toes.

"The car at the park was simply a ruse to scare the American," Natalie explained.

"What about the boat explosion?" Ericka asked. "That incident almost wiped out the royal family."

Natalie shook her head. "That was simply to frighten *you* into going home." So, Ira had been correct. The boat had been aiming at Ericka. "The remote control device was tricky to operate. I would never—"

Natalie's foot slipped. She gasped and with sheer determination clung to the crumbling stone wall. "Nicholas was supposed to marry Larissa. My daughter should have been queen. For that matter *I* should have been queen."

"You?" Nicholas frowned. For a moment he thought the woman was mad. Natalie was a married woman. And then he realized, Natalie was speaking, not about marrying him, but his father. But as far as Nicholas knew there had been nothing between this woman and Zared—but perhaps she'd wanted him. Natalie had always been ambitious. Nicholas wasn't all that surprised to learn she'd aspired to be Vashmira's queen. When his father hadn't been interested, had she become so heartbroken and emotionally damaged that she'd turned against Zared and plotted his assassination?

"I loved your father, Nicholas."

Love and hate were often two sides to the same coin. "Did you kill him?" he demanded, his voice harsh, his throat tight.

"I loved him," Natalie insisted.

"But did you kill him so Larissa would marry me and become queen?"

"I didn't—" Natalie's foot slipped. She teetered on the edge. Screamed. Arms waving, feet kicking, she plunged to her death.

And in that horrible moment, Nicholas knew he would never have the answers he'd sought for so long.

"Oh, God." Ericka flung her arms around him, tears in her eyes. "I'm so sorry. Sorry, she's dead. Sorry, you'll never know for certain if she killed your father."

He hugged Ericka tightly. "For Anton and Larissa, it's better this way. And I have to believe that Natalie was guilty. My father must have disappointed her terribly when he expressed no romantic interest in her. Then she probably pinned all her hopes on Larissa becoming queen."

"And when she finally understood her dream wasn't going to happen, she snapped."

"It's over," Nicholas told Ericka. "It's time to look forward now."

NICHOLAS TOOK A CALL from Anton and then led Ericka to his quarters. She took one look in the dresser mirror at the dirt on her clothes from holding Dimitri and Nikita after they'd come through the secret tunnels and headed straight for the bathroom. "I need a shower, but I want to know why Ira is so positive that Natalie sent the bomb to me."

Nicholas followed her into the bathroom and watched with interest as she kicked off her shoes. "Ira found Natalie's thumb print on the bomb's explosive packaging—not just the timer."

Ericka unbuttoned her filthy blouse and enjoyed the flare of heat in Nicholas' gaze. "You think she told us the truth and really meant only to scare me away?"

"We'll never know for certain. However, she certainly used those secret passages, and she admitted to knowing about the car in the park and the boat on the beach. Whether she expected palace security to intercept the package and stop that bomb from arriving in your quarters, we'll never know." He paused, then continued. "Anton offered his resignation, but I hate to accept it since he knew nothing of his wife's duplicity. He's negotiated a settlement with the Americans and the Israelis. Each party has agreed to accept half of the Russian refugees."

Nicholas reached out and his clever fingers helped her with her blouse buttons, making it difficult for her to concentrate. "And the Russians?"

"Have agreed to let the refugees emigrate."

She shimmied out of her blouse. "What will you do about Anton?"

"How can I fire him when he did nothing wrong except fall in love with the wrong woman?"

She paused in her undressing, hands on her hips. "Are you still worried that I'm the wrong woman for you?"

He bracketed her with his arms against the sink, leaned forward and kissed her forehead, her nose, her mouth. "I cannot change who I am. My past and my mother's actions are a part of me that cannot be changed, and yet…"

"Yes?"

"I cannot imagine you running away from anything. You're the bravest woman I know."

"Lots of things scare me, Nicholas. Like disappointing you."

Nicholas reached into the shower and turned the water to warm. He shot her a rakish grin. "I think I'll join you."

She tugged open his shirt and licked her bottom lip. "Aren't we presumptuous?"

"Tell me about the threat on your laptop," he demanded, and she realized he must have read the message as he'd stepped through the office. In all the excitement over finding the secret passages and Natalie's death, she'd forgotten about the threat against Nicholas and the demand for her to leave him.

Nicholas kept his tone easy, but his eyes narrowed. "When did that message arrive?"

"I'm not sure. I found it on my laptop right before Dimitri and Nikita made their surprise appearance."

He unhooked her bra. "You weren't going to try and leave me and my country out of some misplaced notion that you could save my life by agreeing to this preposterous demand?"

"I considered doing exactly that," she told him truthfully, her voice hitching.

His hands cupped her breasts, his fingers flicking over her sensitive nipples, shooting a rush of pleasure straight to her toes. "But?"

"I can't think when you do that."

He nipped her neck, the tiny bites incredibly erotic.

''It's a new form of inquisition, one I've designed exclusively for you.''

''You mean for your wife?''

Hope flared in his eyes, and a promise that she wouldn't regret her decision. ''Does that mean—?''

''I love you enough to let you risk your neck.'' With her fingertips, she skimmed a path over his shoulder and chest. ''And I'm foolish enough to spend whatever time we have together as husband and wife.''

''It's going to be a long time. A very long time.''

''I'll hold you to that.'' She tilted her head back. ''I do have a condition.''

''I hope you want to marry soon. Tashya told me the Moldovans have agreed to return our crew and plane as a wedding present. We can marry immediately after the coronation ceremony. All the foreign dignitaries will already be here.''

She arched into him, sleek and content and very aware she wanted to make love to this man right now, in the royal shower. ''Well, your need to hurry our engagement should strengthen my negotiating position considerably.''

He grinned. ''I'm in a very good bargaining mood. I suppose you want to run my press corps?''

''Not exactly.''

''You want to see the crown jewels?''

She ran her hand up the inside of his thigh, lingering over the bulge there. ''I've already seen them, and I want exclusive possession.''

''That can be arranged.'' He laughed and slipped off her slacks, then his. He removed a condom from a cabinet. ''What else?''

She plucked the condom from his fingers and tossed it aside. "Children. I want at least two, maybe three."

"I'm ready."

"I can feel that." She snuggled in his arms and tugged his head down until they were nose to nose. "And you have to tell me you love me."

"I do."

"Say it."

"I love you."

NICHOLAS RESTRAINED HIS grin of happiness at the woman who had come to mean so much to him. Their fathers' marriage contract had been a stroke of brilliance. Not only had Nicholas found a queen for his people, he'd found the queen of his heart.

"Can you tell me you love me at least once a day?"

"Twice on Sundays," he agreed.

"Even if you have business on the other side of the world, I expect you to remember your promise."

His pager beeped. He ignored it.

"Shouldn't you answer that?"

He trailed his lips over her mouth, nibbling, teasing, taking. "The only business I'm interested in right now is you."

Voice husky, eyes languid, she grinned at him. "What you're interested in…is funny business."

"That, too." He opened the shower and the sluicing warm water felt cool compared to the heat radiating from his skin. He gathered her into his arms, sharing the spray, ready to share the rest of his life with her, share their children, share a lifetime of love.

Epilogue

Washington Herald

Royal Assassination Attempt Foiled

by Ericka Allen

...The final episode of the mystery of King Zared's assassination ended today with the death of Natalie Belosova. High-level palace sources at the scene remain uncertain whether she accidentally fell from the palace tower or deliberately jumped. Her body was buried in a private ceremony.

The Vashmiran coronation of King Nicholas Zared II and his wedding to this reporter are scheduled for tomorrow. Keeping within the traditions of a true fairy tale, the royal couple plans to live happily ever after.

* * * * *

Chapter One

"Have you ever seen such a radiant bride?" Prince Alexander Zared asked his sister, Princess Tashya.

With an approving smile, Tashya watched her oldest brother, the king of Vashmira, and Ericka, his queen, stroll down the steps of the National Cathedral where his coronation ceremony and their marriage had just taken place. Triumphant music accompanied their footsteps, and thousands of gardenias scented the air as television cameras broadcast the event live to the world.

"Careful, Alexander. If Nicholas catches you so much as sneaking a lingering look at his wife, he'll make you Ambassador to Antarctica."

Not the least perturbed, Alexander grinned. "So you've noticed our dear brother's a bit overprotective of his new bride?"

"He's so in love." Tashya could see the deep emotions in Nicholas' eyes every time he looked at Ericka. She wondered if a man would ever stare at her with such adoration, and if she'd ever respond with the open look of love she saw on Ericka's face. Good for them, Tashya thought. Nicholas deserved some happiness.

Ever since their father's assassination a year ago, Nicholas had taken on much responsibility. Stepping into their father's shoes couldn't have been easy for him. At first, he had balked at accepting an arranged marriage to a stranger, but Vashmiran law had clearly stated that Nicholas must choose a bride before his coronation ceremony. Nicholas and Ericka had only met this past month, yet Tashya suspected Nicholas couldn't have chosen better on his own. Without an arranged marriage, he might never have found a wife at all. In fact, before he'd met Ericka, Tashya's more serious brother had tended to be a workaholic.

However, Nicholas had lucked out and fallen in love with the American. Tashya fully approved—not that anyone had asked for her approval. But she genuinely liked her independent sister-in-law and realized Ericka could help the cause. Tashya intended to seek Queen Ericka's help to establish more equality for women in their country. But that would come later, after the honeymoon. Right now, as they waved to crowds of well-wishers, having the queen at his side was bringing a gentle light of satisfaction to Nicholas' eyes.

Tashya wondered if Alex would ever look so happy. Freed from the pressure of ruling Vashmira, Alexander seemed to drift from woman to woman and party to party. Tall, dark and restless, her brother shifted impatiently from foot to foot, his attention lighting on first a pretty Muslim woman dressed in traditional clothing, then a young blond lady. Eventually he locked gazes with a sophisticated woman sending out unmistakably lustful signals.

Tashya refrained from rolling her eyes. With her luck, the paparazzi would catch her making a face, and she would do nothing to spoil the king's wedding day. Today was going to be perfect.

She discreetly elbowed Alexander in his side. "Perhaps if you stayed with one woman long enough to learn her name, you, too, might fall in love."

Alexander shrugged, his broad shoulders filling out his elegant dress uniform in a way that was sure to increase his already enormous popularity with the ladies. In fact, there had been such wild speculation about who would accompany him to the wedding that he'd chosen to go with his sister, as he often did for official functions.

For her part, Tashya always welcomed her brother's company. Especially since his presence protected her from those men who couldn't see past her title to a living, breathing woman. Sure, she held a title, but that didn't mean she didn't yearn for what other women wanted—a man who loved her for her unique individuality.

Alexander winked at a set of twins, brother and sister, who couldn't be more than four. "I'll never marry."

"Why not?" Tashya waved to the crowd as the bride and groom climbed into a horse-drawn carriage. It took a few minutes for Ericka's attendants to gather and tuck her long train around her feet. With an official handshake, Nicholas thanked each of the young boys accompanying the couple. To each of the little girls, he handed a long-stemmed red rose.

"I like variety. Perhaps the flaw is mine." Alexander's gaze focused on a lovely young woman in the crowd. "I'm distracted so easily."

Tashya nudged him again. "Stop that. She's too young for you."

"I only smiled at her," Alexander said pleasantly, not the least bothered by his sister's tone of disapproval. Alexander's problem was that he expected every woman to love him, and they invariably did. It irked Tashya that while he was never alone, he often seemed lonely. "I may be the perennial bachelor but at least I go out. It wouldn't hurt you to be a little more open to the possibilities," he chided.

"Oh, right. In case you haven't noticed, we still have a double standard in this country. Our people would not accept their princess acting like their prince and going to bed with every—"

"You needn't draw me a mental picture." Alexander had the grace to wince and quickly changed the subject. "Whatever happened between you and the prince of Moldova?"

"The toad?" Tashya shuddered, then waved again before she and Alex finally headed down the steps toward the carriage that awaited. "Absolutely nothing happened between us—that was the problem."

"The man must be blind."

"Oh, he found me attractive enough, all right. In fact, I suspect that's all he wanted. Something pretty to hang on his arm and his every word. Besides, he

had horse breath. Actually, my horses have breath
much sweeter than His Royal High—''

''Okay. Okay. Keep your voice down before you
start another international incident.''

''Nicholas' secretary of state smoothed things
over.''

''But we almost went to war.''

''Surely you don't believe I should have married a
man I thoroughly disliked, so Vashmira would make
an alliance?''

''Nicholas and I hoped you'd be happy with the
Moldovan crown prince. I'm sorry things didn't work
out.''

Alexander helped her into the carriage. They would
parade through the crowds and the city until they
reached the palace and the grand reception hall where
dignitaries and guests from around the world waited.
Vashmira's palace had never looked better and the
aromas wafting from the kitchens this morning had
been heavenly.

Alexander pulled up his trousers slightly to avoid
creasing at the knees before he sat next to her on the
leather seat. Naturally he'd want to look good for the
legions of women he'd dance with at the ball. She,
too, expected to have plenty of partners, but the evening had no appeal for her. She couldn't help worrying
over the logistical nightmare of security.

Just last week Nicholas and Ericka had rooted out
a traitor in their midst. The American government had
responded by sending over a Secret Service team to
guard the royal couple.

Along the parade route, handlers released doves

from cages, and the birds soared into the sky, a sky where dark clouds threatened to block the sun. Tashya leaned back in the carriage seat, closed her eyes, and tipped her face to absorb the last rays of sunlight.

A car backfired, or at least she thought the sound came from a car. People screamed and shouted. She opened her eyes just as Alexander shoved her to the carriage floor.

With an undignified thump, she landed on knees and elbows, her gown riding up her legs. Alexander piled on top of her, pressing her into the carpet.

"What's wrong?" she asked as the carriage driver whipped the horses into a gallop and the milling crowds turned and fled.

"Someone's shooting at us."

"At us?"

Alexander had to be wrong. Neither of them held any power. Who would want to harm them?

"Alex, is some angry husband or father after you?"

"I don't think so."

A shot pinged off the carriage, close to her head. Fear started to wind up her throat and choke off her breath. This was no joke. Someone wasn't just trying to scare them.

Someone was trying to kill them.

HARLEQUIN®
INTRIGUE®

**A royal family in peril...
A kingdom in jeopardy...
And only love can save them!**

THE CROWN
AFFAIR

Continues in November 2002 with

ROYAL RANSOM

BY SUSAN KEARNEY

In the second exciting installment in
THE CROWN AFFAIR trilogy, Princess Tashya's baby
brothers have been kidnapped. With no time to lose,
Her Royal Highness sets out to save the young princes,
whether her family—or the dangerously seductive
CIA agent hired to protect her—liked it or not!

Coming in December 2002:

ROYAL PURSUIT

*Look for these exciting new stories
wherever Harlequin books are sold!*

HARLEQUIN®
Makes any time special ®

FALL IN LOVE
THIS WINTER
WITH
HARLEQUIN BOOKS!

In October 2002 look for these special volumes
led by *USA TODAY* bestselling authors,
and receive MOULIN ROUGE on video*!

*Retail value of $14.98 U.S. Mail-in offer. Two proofs of purchase required.
Limited time offer. Offer expires 3/31/03.

See inside these books for details.

Own MOULIN ROUGE on video!

*This exciting promotion
is available at your
favorite retail outlet.*

Only from

HARLEQUIN®

Makes any time special ®

Princes...Princesses...
London Castles...New York Mansions...
To live the life of a royal!

In 2002, Harlequin Books lets you escape to a world of royalty with these royally themed titles:

Temptation:
January 2002—*A Prince of a Guy* (#861)
February 2002—*A Noble Pursuit* (#865)

American Romance:
The Carradignes: American Royalty (Editorially linked series)
March 2002—*The Improperly Pregnant Princess* (#913)
April 2002—*The Unlawfully Wedded Princess* (#917)
May 2002—*The Simply Scandalous Princess* (#921)
November 2002—*The Inconveniently Engaged Prince* (#945)

Intrigue:
The Carradignes: A Royal Mystery (Editorially linked series)
June 2002—*The Duke's Covert Mission* (#666)

Chicago Confidential
September 2002—*Prince Under Cover* (#678)

The Crown Affair
October 2002—*Royal Target* (#682)
November 2002—*Royal Ransom* (#686)
December 2002—*Royal Pursuit* (#690)

Harlequin Romance:
June 2002—*His Majesty's Marriage* (#3703)
July 2002—*The Prince's Proposal* (#3709)

Harlequin Presents:
August 2002—*Society Weddings* (#2268)
September 2002—*The Prince's Pleasure* (#2274)

Duets:
September 2002—*Once Upon a Tiara/Henry Ever After* (#83)
October 2002—*Natalia's Story/Andrea's Story* (#85)

Celebrate a year of royalty with Harlequin Books!

Available at your favorite retail outlet.

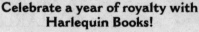

HARLEQUIN®
Makes any time special ®

HSROY02